This second collection of original short stories edited by Maxim Jakubowski includes work by Tanith Lee (whose *Castle of Dark* is also published in *Unicorn*), Jane Gaskell, Paul Ableman and Jessica Amanda Salmonson (a past winner of the World Fantasy Award) amongst others.

Lands of Never is also published in *Unicorn*.

UNICORN

BEYOND LANDS OF NEVER

A FURTHER ANTHOLOGY OF MODERN FANTASY

EDITED BY
MAXIM JAKUBOWSKI

London
UNWIN PAPERBACKS
Boston   Sydney

First published by Unwin Paperbacks 1984

Unwin® Paperbacks
40 Museum Street, London WC1A 1LU, UK

Unwin Paperbacks
Park Lane, Hemel Hempstead, Herts HP2 4TE, UK

George Allen & Unwin Australia Pty Ltd
8 Napier Street, North Sydney, NSW 2060, Australia

British Library Cataloguing in Publication Data

  Beyond lands of never.
1. Fantastic fiction, English
I. Jakubowski, Maxim
823'.01'0815 [FS]   PR1309.F3
ISBN 0-04-823254-8

Type set in 10 on 11½ point Imprint by Computape (Pickering) Ltd
and printed in Great Britain by Cox and Wyman Ltd, Reading

Contents

London-based Tanith Lee is one of the most popular fantasy writers around, particularly with American fans. Her prolific output of adult and juvenile novels is both impressive and imaginative. *Draco, Draco* is not just another story about dragons, as you will see, it is also a tale about a Roman Empire that never was. Watch for the cleverly concealed clues!

Draco, Draco

Tanith Lee

You'll have heard stories, sometimes, of men who have fought and slain dragons. These are all lies. There's no swordsman living ever killed a dragon, though a few swordsmen dead that tried.

On the other hand, I once travelled in company with a fellow who got the name of 'dragon-slayer'.

A riddle? No. I'll tell you.

I was coming from the North back into the South, to civilisation as you may say, when I saw him sitting by the roadside. My first feeling was envy, I admit. He was smart and very clean for someone in the wilds, and he had the South all over him, towns and baths and money. He was crazy, too, because there was gold on his wrists and in one ear. But he had a sharp grey sword, an army sword, so maybe he could defend himself. He was also younger than me, and a great deal prettier, but the last isn't too difficult. I wondered what he'd do when he looked up from his daydream and saw me, tough, dark and sour as a twist of old rope, clopping down on him on my swarthy little horse, ugly as sin, that I love like a daughter.

Then he did look up and I discovered.

'Greetings, stranger. Nice day, isn't it?'

He stayed relaxed as he said it, and somehow you knew from that he really could look after himself. It wasn't he thought I was harmless, just that he thought he could handle me if I tried something. Then again, I had my box of stuff alongside. Most people can tell my trade from that, and the aroma of drugs and herbs. My father was with the Romans, in fact he was probably the last Roman of all, one foot on the ship to go home, the rest of him with my mother up against the barnyard wall. She said he was a camp physician and maybe that was so. Some idea of doctoring grew up with me, though nothing great or grand. An itinerant apothecary is welcome almost anywhere, and can even turn bandits civil. It's not a wonderful life, but it's the only one I know.

I gave the young soldier-dandy that it was a nice day. I added he'd possibly like it better if he hadn't lost his horse.

'Yes, a pity about that. You could always sell me yours.'

'Not your style.'

He looked at her. I could see he agreed. There was also a momentary idea that he might kill me and take her, so I said, 'And she's well known as mine. It would get you a bad name. I've friends round about.' .

He grinned, good-naturedly. His teeth were good, too. What with that, and the hair like barley, and the rest of it – well, he was the kind usually gets what he wants. I was curious as to which army he had hung about with to gain the sword. But since the Eagles flew, there are kingdoms everywhere, chiefs, war-leaders, Roman knights, and every tide brings an invasion up some beach. Under it all, too, you can feel the earth, the actual ground, which had been measured, and ruled with fine roads, the land which had been subdued but never tamed, beginning to quicken. Like the shadows that come with the blowing out of a lamp. Ancient things, which are in my blood somewhere, so I recognise them.

But he was like a new coin that hadn't got dirty yet, nor learned much, though you could see your face in its shine, and cut yourself on its edge.

His name was Caiy. Presently we came to an arrangement and he mounted up behind me on Negra. They spoke a smatter of Latin where I was born, and I called her that before I knew her, for her darkness. I couldn't call her for her hideousness, which is her only other visible attribute.

The fact is, I wasn't primed to the country round that way at all. I'd had word, a day or two prior, that there were Saxons in the area I'd been heading for. And so I switched paths and was soon lost. When I came on Caiy, I'd been pleased with the road, which was Roman, hoping it would go somewhere useful. But, about ten miles after Caiy joined me, the road petered out in a forest. My passenger was lost, too. He was going South, no surprise there, but last night his horse had broken loose and bolted, leaving him stranded. It sounded unlikely, but I wasn't inclined to debate on it. It seemed to me someone might have stolen the horse, and Caiy didn't care to confess.

There was no way round the forest, so we went in and the road died. Being summer, the wolves would be scarce and the bears off in the hills. Nevertheless, the trees had a feel I didn't take to, sombre and still, with the sound of little streams running through like metal chains, and birds that didn't sing but made purrings and clinkings. Negra never baulked nor complained – if I'd waited to call her, I could have done it for her courage and warm-heartedness – but she couldn't come to terms with the forest, either.

'It smells,' said Caiy, who'd been kind enough not to comment on mine, 'as if it's rotting. Or fermenting.'

I grunted. Of course it did, it was, the fool. But the smell told you other things. The centuries, for one. Here were the shadows that had come back when Rome blew out her lamp and sailed away, and left us in the dark.

Then Caiy, the idiot, began to sing to show up the birds who wouldn't. A nice voice, clear and bright. I didn't tell him to leave off. The shadows already knew we were there.

When night came down, the black forest closed like a cellar door.

We made a fire and shared my supper. He'd lost his rations with his mare.

'Shouldn't you tether that – your horse,' suggested Caiy, trying not to insult her since he could see we were partial to each other. 'My mare was tied, but something scared her and she broke the tether and ran. I wonder what it was,' he mused, staring in the fire.

About three hours later, we found out.

I was asleep, and dreaming of one of my wives up in the far North, and she was nagging at me, trying to start a brawl, which she always did for she was taller than me, and liked me to hit her once in a while so she could feel fragile, feminine and mastered. Just as she emptied the beer jar over my head, I heard a sound up in the sky like a storm that was not a storm. And I knew I wasn't dreaming any more.

The sound went over, three or four great claps, and the tops of the forest reeling, and left shuddering. There was a sort of quiver

in the air, as if sediment were stirred up in it. There was even an
extra smell, dank, yet tingling. When the noise was only a
memory, and the bristling hairs began to subside along my body,
I opened my eyes.

Negra was flattened to the ground, her own eyes rolling, but
she was silent. Caiy was on his feet, gawping up at the tree tops
and the strands of starless sky. Then he glared at me.

'What in the name of the Bull was that?'

I noted vaguely that the oath showed he had Mithraic alle-
giances, which generally meant Roman. Then I sat up, rubbed
my arms and neck to get human, and went to console Negra.
Unlike his silly cavalry mare she hadn't bolted.

'It can't,' he said, 'have been a bird. Though I'd have sworn
something flew over.'

'No, it wasn't a bird.'

'But it had wings. Or – no, it couldn't have had wings the size of
that.'

'Yes it could. They don't carry it far, is all.'

'Apothecary, stop being so damned provoking. If you know,
out with it! Though I don't see how you can know. And don't tell
me it's some bloody woods demon I won't believe in.'

'Nothing like that,' I said. 'It's real enough. Natural, in its own
way. Not,' I amended, 'that I ever came across one before, but
I've met some who did.'

Caiy was going mad, like a child working up to a tantrum.
'*Well?*'

I suppose he had charmed and irritated me enough I wanted to
retaliate, because I just quoted some bastard nonsensical jabber-
Latin chant at him:

Bis terribilis –
Bis appellare –
Draco! Draco!

At least, it made him sit down.

'What?' he eventually said.

At my age I should be over such smugness. I said,

'It was a dragon.'

Caiy laughed. But he had glimpsed it, and knew better than I
did that I was right.

Nothing else happened that night. In the morning we started off again and there was a rough track, and then the forest began to thin out. After a while we emerged on the crown of a moor. The land dropped down to a valley, and on the other side there were sunny smoky hills and a long streamered sky. There was something else, too.

Naturally, Caiy said it first, as if everything new always surprised him, as if we hadn't each of us, in some way, been waiting for it, or something like it.

'This place stinks.'

'Hn.'

'Don't just grunt at me, you blasted quack doctor. It does, doesn't it? Why?'

'Why do you think?'

He brooded, pale gold and citified, behind me. Negra tried to paw the ground, and then made herself desist.

Neither of us brave humans had said any more about what had interrupted sleep in the forest, but when I'd told him no dragon could fly far on its wings, for from all I'd ever heard they were too large and only some freakish lightness in their bones enabled them to get airborne at all, I suppose we had both taken it to heart. Now here were the valley and the hills, and here was this reek lying over everything, strange, foul, alien, comparable to nothing, really. Dragon smell.

I considered. No doubt, the dragon went on an aerial patrol most nights, circling as wide as it could, to see what might be there for it. There were other things I'd learnt. These beasts hunt nocturnally, like cats. At the same time, a dragon is more like a crow in its habits. It will attack and kill, but normally it eats carrion, dead things, or dying and immobilised. It's light, as I said, it has to be to take the skies, but the lack of weight is compensated by the armour, the teeth and talons. Then again, I'd heard of dragons that breathed fire. I've never been quite convinced there. It seems more likely to me such monsters only live in volcanic caves, the mountain itself belching flame and the dragon taking credit for it. Maybe not. But certainly, this dragon was no fire-breather. The ground would have been scorched for miles; I've listened to stories where that happened. There were no marks of fire. Just the insidious pervasive stench that I knew, by the time we'd gone down into the valley, would be so familiar, so soaked into us, we would hardly notice it any more, or the scent of anything else.

I awarded all this information to my passenger. There followed a long verbal delay. I thought he might just be flabbergasted at getting so much chat from me, but then he said, very hushed, 'You truly believe all this, don't you?'

I didn't bother with the obvious, just clucked to Negra, trying to make her turn back the way we'd come. But she was unsure and for once unco-operative, and suddenly his strong hand, the nails groomed even now, came down on my arm.

'Wait, Apothecary. If it *is* true – '

'Yes, yes,' I said. I sighed. 'You want to go and challenge it, and become a hero.' He held himself like marble, as if I were speaking of some girl he thought he loved. I didn't see why I should waste experience and wisdom on him, but then. 'No man ever killed a dragon. They're plated, all over, even the underbelly. Arrows and spears just bounce off – even a pilum. Swords clang and snap in half. Yes, yes,' I reiterated, 'you've heard of men who slashed the tongue, or stabbed into an eye. Let me tell you, if they managed to reach that high and actually did it, then they just made the brute angry. Think of the size and shape of a dragon's head, the way the pictures show it. It's one hell of a push from the eye into the brain. And you know, there's one theory the eyelid is armoured, too, and can come down faster than *that*.'

'Apothecary,' he said. He sounded dangerous. I just knew what he must look like. Handsome, noble and insane.

'Then I won't keep you,' I said. 'Get down and go on and the best of luck.'

I don't know why I bothered. I should have tipped him off and ridden for it, though I wasn't sure Negra could manage to react sufficiently fast, she was that edgy. Anyway, I didn't, and sure enough next moment his sword was at the side of my throat, and so sharp it had drawn blood.

'You're the clever one,' he said, 'the know-all. And you do seem to know more than I do, about this. So you're my guide, and your scruff-bag of a horse, if it even deserves the name, is my transport. Giddy-up, the pair of you.'

That was that. I never argue with a drawn sword. The dragon

would be lying up by day, digesting and dozing, and by night I could hole up someplace myself. Tomorrow Caiy would be dead and I could leave. And I would, of course, have seen a dragon for myself.

After an hour and a half's steady riding – better once I'd persuaded him to switch from the sword to poking a dagger against my ribs, less tiring for us both – we came around a stand of woods, and there was a village. It was the savage Northern kind, thatch and wattle and turf banks, but big for all that, a good mile of it, not all walled. There were walls this end, however, and men on the gate, peering at us.

Caiy was aggrieved because he was going to have to ride up to them pillion, but he knew better now than to try managing Negra alone. He maybe didn't want to pretend she was his horse in any case.

As we pottered up the pebbled track to the gate, he sprang off and strode forward, arriving before me, and began to speak.

When I got closer I heard him announcing, in his dramatic, beautiful voice,

' – And if it's a fact, I swear by the Victory of the Light that I will meet the thing and kill it.'

They were muttering. The dragon smell, even though we were used to it, sodden with it, seemed more acid here. Poor Negra had been voiding herself from sheer terror all up the path. With fortune on our side, there would be somewhere below ground, some cave or dug out place, where they'd be putting their animals out of the dragon's way, and she could shelter with the others.

Obviously, the dragon hadn't always been active in this region. They'd scarcely have built their village if it had. No, it would have been like the tales. Dragons live for centuries. They can sleep for centuries, too. Unsuspecting, man moves in, begins to till and build and wax prosperous. Then the dormant dragon wakes under the hill. They're like the volcanoes I spoke of, in that. Which is perhaps, more than habitat, why so many of the legends say they breathe fire when they wake.

The interesting thing was, even clouded by the dragon stink, initially, the village didn't seem keen to admit to anything.

Caiy, having made up his mind to accept the dragon – and afraid of being wrong – started to rant. The men at the gate were frightened and turning nasty. Leading Negra now, I approached, tapped my chest of potions and said:

'Or, if you don't want your dragon slain, I can cure some of your other troubles. I've got medicines for almost everything. Boils, warts. Ear pains. Tooth pains. Sick eyes. Women's afflictions. I have here – '

'Shut up, you toad-turd,' said Caiy.

One of the guards suddenly laughed. The tension sagged.

Ten minutes after, we had been let in the gate and were trudging through the cow-dung and wild flowers – neither of which were to be smelled through the other smell – to the headman's hall.

It was around two hours after that when we found out why the appearance of a rescuing champion-knight had given them the jitters.

It seemed they had gone back to the ancient way, propitiation, the scapegoat. For three years, they had been making an offering to the dragon, in spring, and at midsummer, when it was likely to be most frisky.

Anyone who knew dragons from a book would tell them this wasn't the way. But they knew their dragon from myth. Every time they made sacrifice, they imagined the thing could understand and appreciate what they'd done for it, and would therefore be more amenable.

In reality, of course, the dragon had never attacked the village. It had thieved cattle off the pasture by night, elderly or sick cows at that, and lambs that were too little and weak to run. It would have taken people, too, but only those who were disabled and alone. I said, a dragon is lazy and prefers carrion, or what's defenceless. Despite being big, they aren't so big they'd go after a whole tribe of men. And though even forty men together undoubtedly couldn't wound a dragon, they could exhaust it, if they kept up a rough-house. Eventually it would keel over and they could brain it. You seldom hear of forty men going off in a band to take a dragon, however. Dragons are still ravelled up with night fears and spiritual mysteries, and latterly with an Eastern superstition of a mighty demon who can assume the form of a dragon which is invincible and – naturally – breathes sheer flame. So, this village, like many another, would put out its sacrifice, one girl tied to a post, and leave her there, and the dragon would have her. Why not? She was helpless, fainting with horror – and young and tender into the bargain. Perfect. You never could convince them that, instead of appeasing the monster, the sacrifice encourages it to stay. Look at it from the dragon's point of view. Not only are there dead sheep and stray cripples to devour, but once in a while a nice juicy damsel on a stick. Dragons don't think like a man, but they do have memories.

When Caiy realised what they were about to do, tonight, as it turned out, he went red then white, exactly as they do in a bardic lay. Not anger, mind you. He didn't comprehend anymore than they did. It was merely the awfulness of it.

He stood up and chose a stance, quite unconsciously impress-ive, and assured us he'd save her. He swore to it in front of us all, the chieftain, his men, me. And he swore it by the Sun, so I knew he meant business.

They were scared, but now also childishly hopeful. It was part of their mythology again. All mythology seems to take this tack somewhere, the dark against the light, the Final Battle. It's rot, but there.

Following a bit of drinking to seal the oath, they cheered up and the chief ordered a feast. Then they took Caiy to see the chosen sacrifice.

Her name was Niemeh, or something along those lines.

She was sitting in a little lamplit cell off the hall. She wasn't fettered, but a warrior stood guard beyond the screen, and there was no window. She had nothing to do except weave flowers together, and she was doing that, making garlands for her death procession in the evening.

When Caiy saw her, his colour drained away again.

He stood and stared at her, while somebody explained he was her champion.

Though he got on my nerves, I didn't blame him so much this time. She was about the most beautiful thing I ever hope to see. Young, obviously, and slim, but with a woman's shape, if you have my meaning, and long hair more fair even than Caiy's, and green eyes like sea pools and a face like one of the white flowers in her hands, and a sweet mouth.

I looked at her as she listened gravely to all they said. I

remembered how in the legends it's always the loveliest and the most gentle gets picked for the dragon's dinner. You perceive the sense in the gentle part. A girl with a temper might start a ruckus.

When Caiy had been introduced and once more sworn by the Sun to slay the dragon and so on, she thanked him. If things had been different, she would have blushed and trembled, excited by Caiy's attention. But she was past all that. You could see, if you looked, she didn't believe anyone could save her. But though she must have been half dead already of despair and fright, she still made space to be courteous.

Then she glanced over Caiy's head straight at me, and she smiled so I wouldn't feel left out.

'And who is this man?' she asked.

They all looked startled, having forgotten me. Then someone who had warts recalled I'd said I could fix him something for warts, and told her I was the apothecary.

A funny little shiver went through her then.

She was so young and so pretty. If I'd been Caiy I'd have stopped spouting rubbish about the dragon. I'd have found some way to lay out the whole village, and grabbed her, and gone. But that would have been a stupid thing to do, too. I've enough of the old blood to know about such matters. She was the sacrifice and she was resigned to it; more, she didn't dream she could be anything else. I've come across rumours, here and there, of girls, men too, chosen to die, who escaped. But the fate stays on them. Hide them securely miles off, across water, beyond tall hills, still they feel the geas weigh like lead upon their souls. They kill themselves in the end, or go mad. And this girl, this Niemeh, you could see it in her. No, I would never have abducted her. It would have been no use. She was convinced she must die, as if she'd seen it written in light on a stone, and maybe she had.

She returned to her garlands, and Caiy, tense as a bowstring, led us back to the hall.

Meat was roasting and more drink came out and more talk came out. You can kill anything as often as you like, that way.

It wasn't a bad feast, as such up-country things go. But all through the shouts and toasts and guzzlings, I kept thinking of her in her cell behind the screen, hearing the clamour and aware of this evening's sunset, and how it would be to die ... as she would have to. I didn't begin to grasp how she could bear it.

By late afternoon they were mostly sleeping it off, only Caiy had had the sense to go and sweat the drink out with soldiers' exercises in the yard, before a group of sozzled admirers of all sexes.

When someone touched my shoulder, I thought it was Warty after his cure, but no. It was the guard from the girl's cell, who said very low, 'She says she wants to speak to you. Will you come, now?'

I got up and went with him. I had a spinning minute, wondering if perhaps she didn't believe she must die after all, and would appeal to me to save her. But in my heart of hearts I guessed it wasn't that.

There was another man blocking the entrance, but they let me go in alone, and there Niemeh sat, making garlands yet, under her lamp.

But she looked up at me, and her hands fell like two more white flowers on the flowers in her lap. 'I need some medicine, you see,' she said. 'But I can't pay you. I don't have anything. Although my uncle – '

'No charge,' I said hurriedly.

She smiled. 'It's for tonight.'

'Oh,' I said.

'I'm not brave,' she said, 'but it's worse than just being afraid. I know I shall die. That it's needful. But part of me wants to live so much – my reason tells me one thing but my body won't listen. I'm frightened I shall panic, struggle and scream and weep – I don't want that. It isn't right. I have to consent, or the sacrifice isn't any use. Do you know about that?'

'Oh, yes,' I said.

'I thought so. I thought you did. Then ... can you give me something, a medicine or herb – so I shan't feel anything? I don't mean the pain. That doesn't matter. The gods can't blame me if I cry out then, they wouldn't expect me to be beyond pain. But only to make me not care, not want to live so very much.'

'An easy death.'

'Yes.' She smiled again. She seemed serene and beautiful. 'Oh, yes.'

I looked at the floor.

'The soldier. Maybe he'll kill it,' I said.

She didn't say anything.

When I glanced up, her face wasn't serene any more. It was brimful of terror. Caiy would have been properly insulted.

'Is it you can't give me anything? Don't you have anything? I was sure you did. That you were sent here to me to – to help, so I shouldn't have to go through it all alone – '

'There,' I said, 'it's all right. I do have something. Just the thing. I keep it for women in labour when the child's slow and hurting them. It works a treat. They go sort of misty and far off, as if they were nearly asleep. It'll dull pain, too. Even – any kind of pain.'

'Yes,' she whispered, 'I should like that.' And then she caught my hand and kissed it. 'I knew you would,' she said, as if I'd promised her the best and loveliest thing in all the earth. Another man, it would have broken him in front of her. But I'm harder than most.

When she let me, I retrieved my hand, nodded reassuringly, and went out. The chieftain was awake and genial enough, so I had a word with him. I told him what the girl had asked. 'In the East,' I said, 'it's the usual thing, give them something to help them through. They call it Nektar, the drink of the gods. She's consented,' I said, 'but she's very young and scared, delicately bred too. You can't grudge her this.' He acquiesced immediately, as glad as she was, as I'd hoped. It's a grim affair, I should imagine, when the girl shrieks for pity all the way up to the hills. I hadn't thought there'd be any problem. On the other hand, I hadn't wanted to be caught slipping her potions behind anyone's back.

I mixed the drug in the cell where she could watch. She was interested in everything I did, the way the condemned are nearly always interested in every last detail, even how a cobweb hangs.

I made her promise to drink it all, but none of it until they came to bring her out. 'It may not last otherwise. You don't want it to wear off before – too early.'

'No,' she said. 'I'll do exactly what you say.'

When I was going out again, she said, 'If I can ask them for anything for you, the gods, when I meet them ... '

It was in my mind to say: Ask them to go stick — but I didn't. She was trying to keep intact her trust in recompense, immortality. I said, 'Just ask them to look after you.'

She had such a sweet, sweet mouth. She was made to love and be loved, to have children and sing songs and die when she was old, peacefully, in her sleep.

And there would be others like her. The dragon would be given those, too. Eventually, it wouldn't just be maidens, either. The taboo states it has to be a virgin so as to safeguard any unborn life. Since a virgin can't be with child — there's one religion says different, I forget which — they stipulate virgins. But in the end any youthful woman, who can reasonably be reckoned as not with child, will do. And then they go on to the boys. Which is the most ancient sacrifice there is.

I passed a very young girl in the hall, trotting round with the beer-dipper. She was comely and innocent, and I recollected I'd seen her earlier and asked myself, Are you the next? And who'll be next after you?

Niemeh was the fifth. But, I said, dragons live a long while. And the sacrifices always get to be more frequent. Now it was twice a year. In the first year it had been once. In a couple more years it would happen at every season, with maybe three victims in the summer when the creature was most active.

And in ten more years it would be every month, and they'd have learned to raid other villages to get girls and young men to give it, and there would be a lot of bones about, besides, fellows like Caiy, dragon-slayers dragon slain.

I went after the girl with the beer-dipper and drained it. But drink never did comfort me much.

And presently, it would be time to form the procession and start for the hills.

It was the last gleaming golden hour of day when we set off.

The valley was fertile and sheltered. The westering light caught and flashed in the trees and out of the streams. Already there was a sort of path stamped smooth and kept clear of undergrowth. It would have been a pleasant journey, if they'd been going anywhere else.

There was sunlight warm on the sides of the hills, too. The sky was almost cloudless, transparent. If it hadn't been for the tainted air, you would never have thought anything was wrong. But the track wound up the first slope and around, and up again, and there, about a hundred yards off, was the flank of a bigger hill that went down into shadow at its bottom, and never took the sun. That underside was bare of grass, and eaten out in caves, one cave larger than the rest and very black, with a strange black stillness, as if light and weather and time itself stopped just inside. Looking at that, you'd know at once, even with sun on your face and the whole lucid sky above.

They'd brought her all this way in a Roman litter which somehow had become the property of the village. It had lost its roof and its curtains, just a kind of cradle on poles, but Niemeh had sat in it on their shoulders, motionless, and dumb. I had only stolen one look at her, to be sure, but her face had turned mercifully blank and her eyes were opaque. What I'd given her started its work swiftly. She was beyond us all now. I was only anxious everything else would occur before her condition changed.

Her bearers set the litter down and lifted her out. They'd have to support her, but they would know about that, girls with legs gone to water, even passed out altogether. And I suppose the ones who fought and screamed would be forced to sup strong ale, or else concussed with a blow.

Everyone walked a little more, until we reached a natural palisade of rock. This spot provided concealment, while over-looking the cave and the ground immediately below it. There was a stagnant dark pond caught in the gravel there, but on our side, facing the cave, a patch of clean turf with a post sticking up, about the height of a tall man.

The two warriors supporting Niemeh went on with her towards the post. The rest of us stayed behind the rocks, except for Caiy.

We were all garlanded with flowers. Even I had had to be, and I hadn't made a fuss. What odds? But Caiy wasn't garlanded. He was the one part of the ritual which, though arcanely acceptable, was still profane. And that was why, even though they would let him attack the dragon, they had nevertheless brought the girl to appease it.

There was some kind of shackle at the post. It wouldn't be iron, because anything fey has an allergy to sable metals, even so midnight a thing as a dragon. Bronze, probably. They locked one part around her waist and another round her throat. Only the teeth and claws could get her out of her bonds now, piece by piece.

She sagged forward in the toils. She seemed unconscious at last, and I wanted her to be.

The two men hurried back, up the slope and into the rock cover with the rest of us. Sometimes the tales have the people rush away when they've put out their sacrifice, but usually the people stay, to witness. It's quite safe. The dragon won't go after them with something tasty chained up right under its nose.

Caiy didn't remain beside the post. He moved down towards the edge of the polluted pond. His sword was drawn. He was quite ready. Though the sun couldn't get into the hollow to fire his hair or the metal blade, he cut a grand figure, heroically braced there between the maiden and Death.

At the end, the day spilled swiftly. Suddenly all the shoulders of the hills grew dim, and the sky became the colour of lavender, and then a sort of mauve amber, and the stars broke through.

There was no warning.

I was looking at the pond, where the dragon would come to drink, judging the amount of muck there seemed to be in it. And suddenly there was a reflection in the pond, from above. It wasn't definite, and it was upside down, but even so my heart plummeted through my guts.

There was a feeling behind the rock, the type you get, they tell me, in the battle lines, when the enemy appears. And mixed with this, something of another feeling, more maybe like the inside of some god's house when they call on him, and he seems to come.

I forced myself to look then, at the cave mouth. This, after all, was the evening I would see a real dragon, something to relate to others, as others had related such things to me.

It crept out of the cave, inch by inch, nearly down on its belly, cat-like.

The sky wasn't dark yet, a Northern dusk seems often endless. I could see well, and better and better as the shadow of the cave fell away and the dragon advanced into the paler shadow by the pond.

At first, it seemed unaware of anything but itself and the

twilight. It flexed and stretched itself. There was something uncanny, even in such simple movements, something evil. And timeless.

The Romans know an animal they call Elephantus, and I mind an ancient clerk in one of the towns describing this beast to me, fairly accurately, for he'd seen one once. The dragon wasn't as large as elephantus, I should say. Actually not that much higher than a fair-sized cavalry gelding, if rather longer. But it was sinuous, more sinuous than any snake. The way it crept and stretched and flexed, and curled and slewed its head, its skeleton seemed fluid.

There are plenty of mosaics, paintings. It was like that, the way men have shown them from the beginning. Slender, tapering to the elongated head, which is like a horse's, too, and not like, and to the tail, though it didn't have that spade-shaped sting they put on them sometimes, like a scorpion's. There were spines, along the tail and the back-ridge, and the neck and head. The ears were set back, like a dog's. Its legs were short, but that didn't make it seem ungainly. The ghastly fluidity was always there, not grace, but something so like grace it was nearly unbearable.

It looked almost the colour the sky was now, slatey, bluish-grey, like metal but dull; the great overlapping plates of its scales had no burnish. Its eyes were black and you didn't see them, and then they took some light from somewhere, and they flared like two flat coins, cat's eyes, with nothing – no brain, no soul – behind them.

It had been going to drink, but had scented something more interesting than dirty water, which was the girl.

The dragon stood there, static as a rock, staring at her over the pond. Then gradually its two wings, that had been folded back like fans along its sides, opened and spread.

They were huge, those wings, much bigger than the rest of it. You could see how it might be able to fly with them. Unlike the body, there were no scales, only skin, membrane, with ribs of external bone. Bat's wings, near enough. It seemed feasible a sword could go through them, damage them, but that would only maim, and all too likely they were tougher than they seemed.

Then I left off considering. With its wings spread like that, unused – like a crow – it began to sidle around the water, the blind coins of eyes searing on the post and the sacrifice.

Somebody shouted. My innards sprang over. Then I realised it was Caiy. The dragon had nearly missed him, so intent it was on the feast, so he had had to call it.

Bis terribilis – Bis appellare – Draco! Draco!

I'd never quite understood that antic chant, and the Latin was execrable. But I think it really means to know a dragon exists is bad enough, to call its name and summon it – call twice, twice terrible – is the notion of a maniac.

The dragon wheeled. It – *flowed*. Its elongated horse's-head-which-wasn't was before him, and Caiy's sharp sword slashed up and down and bit against the jaw. It happened, what they say – sparks shot glittering in the air. Then the head split, not from any wound, just the chasm of the mouth. It made a sound at him, not a hissing, a sort of *hroosh*. Its breath would be poisonous, almost as bad as fire. I saw Caiy stagger at it, and then one of the long feet on the short legs went out through the gathering dark. The blow looked slow and harmless. It threw Caiy thirty feet, right across the pond. He fell at the entrance to the cave, and lay quiet. The sword was still in his hand. His grip must have clamped down on it involuntarily. He'd likely bitten his tongue as well, in the same way.

The dragon looked after him, you could see it pondering whether to go across again and dine. But it was more attracted by the other morsel it had smelled first. It knew from its scent this was the softer more digestible flesh. And so it ignored Caiy, leaving him for later, and eddied on towards the post, lowering its head as it came, the light leaving its eyes.

I looked. The night was truly blooming now, but I could see, and the darkness didn't shut my ears; there were sounds, too. You weren't there, and I'm not about to try to make you see and hear what I did. Niemeh didn't cry out. She was senseless by then, I'm sure of it. She didn't feel or know any of what it did to her. Afterwards, when I went down with the others, there wasn't much left. It even carried some of her bones into the cave with it, to chew. Her garland was lying on the ground since the dragon had no interest in garnish. The pale flowers were no longer pale.

She had consented, and she hadn't had to endure it. I've seen things as bad that had been done by men, and for men there's no excuse. And yet, I never hated a man as I hated the dragon, a loathing, deadly, sickening hate.

The moon was rising when it finished. It went again to the pond, and drank deeply. Then it moved up the gravel back towards the cave. It paused beside Caiy, sniffed him, but there was no hurry. Having fed so well, it was sluggish. It stepped into the pitch-black hole of the cave, and drew itself from sight, inch by inch, as it had come out, and was gone.

Presently Caiy pulled himself off the ground, first to his hands and knees, then on to his feet.

We, the watchers, were amazed. We'd thought him dead, his back broken, but he had only been stunned, as he told us afterwards. Not even stunned enough not to have come to, dazed and unable to rise, before the dragon quite finished its feeding. He was closer than any of us. He said it maddened him – as if he hadn't been mad already – and so, winded and part stupefied as he was, he got up and dragged himself into the dragon's cave after it. And this time he meant to kill it for sure, no matter what it did to him.

Nobody had spoken a word, up on our rocky place, and no one spoke now. We were in a kind of communion, a trance. We leaned forward and gazed at the black gape in the hill where they had both gone.

Maybe a minute later, the noises began. They were quite extraordinary, as if the inside of the hill itself were gurning and sharling. But it was the dragon, of course. Like the stink of it, those sounds it made were untranslatable. I could say it looked this way comparable to an elephantus, or that way to a cat, a horse, a bat. But the cries and roars – no. They were like nothing else I've heard in the world, or been told of. There were, however, other noises, as of some great heap of things disturbed. And stones rattling, rolling.

The villagers began to get excited or hysterical. Nothing like this had happened before. Sacrifice is usually predictable.

They stood, and started to shout, or groan and invoke supernatural protection. And then a silence came from inside the hill, and silence returned to the villagers.

I don't remember how long it went on. It seemed like months.

Then suddenly something moved in the cave mouth.

There were yells of fear. Some of them took to their heels, but came back shortly when they realised the others were rooted to the spot, pointing and exclaiming, not in anguish but awe. That was because it was Caiy, and not the dragon, that had emerged from the hill.

He walked like a man who has been too long without food and water, head bowed, shoulders drooping, legs barely able to hold him up. He floundered through the edges of the pond and the sword trailed from his hand in the water. Then he tottered over the slope and was right before us. He somehow raised his head then, and got out the sentence no one had ever truly reckoned to hear.

'It's – dead,' said Caiy, and slumped unconscious in the moonlight.

They used the litter to get him to the village, as Niemeh didn't need it any more.

We hung around the village for nearly ten days. Caiy was his merry self by the third, and since there had been no sign of the dragon, by day or night, a party of them went up to the hills, and, kindling torches at noon, slunk into the cave to be sure.

It was dead all right. The stench alone would have verified that, a different perfume than before, and all congealed there, around the cave. In the valley, even on the second morning, the live dragon smell was almost gone. You could make out goats and hay and mead and unwashed flesh and twenty varieties of flowers.

I myself didn't go in the cave. I went only as far as the post. I understood it was safe, but I just wanted to be there once more, where the few bones that were Niemeh had fallen through the shackles to the earth. And I can't say why, for you can explain nothing to bones.

There was rejoicing and feasting. The whole valley was full of it. Men came from isolated holdings, cots and huts, and a rough-looking lot they were. They wanted to glimpse Caiy the dragon-slayer, to touch him for luck and lick the finger. He laughed. He hadn't been badly hurt, and but for bruises was as right as rain, up in the hayloft half the time with willing girls, who would afterwards boast their brats were sons of the hero. Or else he was blind drunk in the chieftain's hall.

In the end, I collected Negra, fed her apples and told her she was the best horse in the land, which she knows is a lie and not what I say the rest of the time. I had sound directions now, and was planning to ride off quietly and let Caiy go on as he desired, but I was only a quarter of a mile from the village when I heard the splayed tocking of horse's hooves. Up he galloped beside me on a decent enough horse, the queen of the chief's stable, no doubt, and grinning, with two beer skins.

I accepted one, and we continued, side by side.

'I take it you're sweet on the delights of my company,' I said at last, an hour after, when the forest was in view over the moor.

'What else, Apothecary? Even my insatiable lust to steal your gorgeous horse has been removed. I now have one of my very own, if not a third as beautiful.' Negra cast him a sidelong look as if she would like to bite him. But he paid no attention. We trotted on for another mile or so before he added, 'And there's something I want to ask you, too.'

I was wary, and waited to find out what came next.

Finally, he said, 'You must know a thing or two in your trade about how bodies fit together. That dragon, now. You seemed to know all about dragons.'

I grunted. Caiy didn't cavil at the grunt. He began idly to describe how he'd gone into the cave, a tale he had flaunted a mere three hundred times in the chieftain's hall. But I didn't cavil either, I listened carefully.

The cave entry-way was low and vile, and soon it opened into a cavern. There was elf-light, more than enough to see by, and water running here and there along the walls and over the stony floor.

There in the cavern's centre, glowing now like filthy silver, lay the dragon, on a pile of junk such as dragons always accumulate. They're like crows and magpies in that, also, shiny things intrigue them and they take them to their lairs to paw possessively and to lie on. The rumours of hoards must come from this, but usually the collection is worthless, snapped knives, impure glass that had sparkled under the moon, rusting armlets from some victim, and all of it soiled by the devil's droppings, and muddled up with split bones.

When he saw it like this, I'd bet the hero's reckless heart failed him. But he would have done his best, to stab the dragon in the eye, the root of the tongue, the vent under the tail, as it clawed him in bits.

'But you see,' Caiy now said to me, 'I didn't have to.'

This, of course, he hadn't said in the hall. No. He had told the village the normal things, the lucky lunge and the brain pierced, and the death throes, which we'd all heard plainly enough. If anyone noticed his sword had no blood on it, well, it had trailed in the pond, had it not?

'You see,' Caiy went on, 'it was lying there comatose one minute, and then it began to writhe about, and to go into a kind of spasm. Something got dislodged off the hoard-pile – a piece of cracked-up armour, I think, gilded – and knocked me silly again. And when I came round, the dragon was all sprawled about, and dead as yesterday's roast mutton.'

'Hn,' I said. '*Hn*n.'

'The point being,' said Caiy, watching the forest and not me, 'I must have done something to it with the first blow, outside. Dislocated some bone or other. You told me their bones have no marrow. So to do that might be conceivable. A fortunate stroke. But it took a while for the damage to kill it.'

'Hn*n*.'

'Because,' said Caiy, softly, 'you do believe I killed it, don't you?'

'In the legends,' I said, 'they always do.'

'But you said before that, in reality, a man can't kill a dragon.'

'One did,' I said.

'Something I managed outside then. Brittle bones. That first blow to its skull.'

'Very likely.'

Another silence. Then he said:

'Do you have any gods, Apothecary?'

'Maybe.'

'Will you swear me an oath by them, and then call me "dragon-slayer"? Put it another way. You've been a help. I don't like to turn on my friends. Unless I have to.'

His hand was nowhere near that honed sword of his, but the sword was in his eyes and his quiet, oh-so-easy voice. He had his reputation to consider, did Caiy. But I've no reputation at all. So I swore my oath and I called him dragon-slayer, and when our roads parted my hide was intact. He went off to glory somewhere I'd never want to go.

Well, I've seen a dragon, and I do have gods. But I told them, when I swore that oath, I'd almost certainly break it, and my gods are accustomed to me. They don't expect honour and chivalry. And there you are.

Caiy never killed the dragon. It was Niemeh, poor lovely loving gentle Niemeh who killed it. In my line of work, you learn about your simples. Which cure, which bring sleep, which bring the long sleep without awakening. There are some miseries in this blessed world can only end in death, and the quicker death the better. I told you I was a hard man. I couldn't save her, I gave you reasons why. But there were all those others who would have followed her. Other Niemeh's. Other Caiy's, for that matter. I gave her enough in the cup to put out the life of fifty strong men. It didn't pain her, and she didn't show she was dead before she had to be. The dragon devoured her, and with her the drug I'd dosed her with. And so Caiy earned the name of dragon-slayer.

And it wasn't a riddle.

And no, I haven't considered making a profession of it. Once is enough with any twice-terrible thing. Heroes and knights need their impossible challenges. I'm not meant for any bard's romantic song, a look will tell you that. You won't ever find me in the Northern hills calling 'Draco! Draco!'

Since her debut at a fantastically young age with her well-known Atlantean series of novels, Jane Gaskell has been somewhat quiet in the publishing field. This is due to her full-time journalistic involvement with London's *Daily Mail*. The following, likely to prove controversial, story is her first in many years and is excerpted from a novel in progress.

Caves

Jane Gaskell

Julia could not see the blanket of fields and woods over which the eagle carried her. Her eyes were full of tears. Of terror, of shock, of flapping air and vastness and vertigo.

It was thus not like flight at all. Julia had, of course, imagined flight when her flying friends boasted of it. Flight had seemed an attractive concept. It had denoted freedom, probably. Julia had thought of gliding, floating, being in control without feeling weighty.

But this, now. This was real, high and windy and real, and like all real things it was not a patch on the imagined or the play. Also, like all real things, it did actually get her somewhere.

Julia as a passenger, the eagle on automatic pilot, were passing over the volcanic valleys of the Giants of this territory. Julia could not see the valleys, so full were her eyes of the tears of reality. She could not even smell them, so frightened and sad was she, till she was plunged right down into the sulphurous chimney of a giant rift. The Eagle had been shot by a Giant's arquebus.

The eagle was brazen, and had no heart. But though an ordinary archer could never have met a mark on the thing's scorching flight-path, the Giant with the great magnetically fletched arrows was no ordinary archer.

The eagle beat its heartless wings. To no avail. It was plunged, down down into the sulphur and the reek.

The Giant was very big. So were all his brothers. He had tusks, some flat and yellowish with darker grooves in them. Some of his tusks were longer, and jutted out from his upper lip. He caught the eagle without staggering much. He ripped off its beating pinion, revealing the raw machinery. The eagle cried out.

The Giant had two right arms and two left arms. With one left arm (he was left handed) he held the rattling groaning eagle, while with his other left hand and his two right arms he proceeded to pull out the internal engine.

The eagle's talons had tightened dreadfully on Julia at the initial capture. But as the crucial inwards of the eagle were pulled out of it, its grip on Julia relaxed. She was absolutely alert, ready to dart in one smooth move to a shadowy corner she thought near enough and dark enough. It was her very intensity of stillness or just simply her very intensity, which drew the glance of the Giant.

'What then have we here?' he asked in true Giant style.

His voice was a roaring in Julia's ears: it vibrated around her body and set trembling any loose bits, such as her hair and her little breasts.

He picked her up very delicately, in fingers and thumb, and set her on the lower of his right palms. He knelt to contemplate her, bringing his depth-charged gaze fairly close the better to contemplate her. Julia had not tried to run. She felt it would be impractical, since in reaching for her (and how much reach he had) he could grab and pionion her too tightly, which for her ribcage or pelvis could be disaster, no concern of his: or, say she reached or almost reached the desired shadow, he might make even just one step in search of her, and that step might crush her.

But most of all, if truth be told, Julia wanted not to lose dignity with this monster. For if you lose dignity with such a captor, she felt, you lose any comfort or rhythm which might otherwise embellish your own death.

The Giant's countenance so close to Julia at this first encounter did not yet terrify her.

She could not yet piece the features together as any whole expression. She had to look from eye to eye for instance, to see how the look of each affected the look of the other. Then the mouth attracted her attention. The set of it: that was as interesting in relation to the set of the two eyes. The tusks jutted, but not, at this very moment, aggressively.

The fingers of the other right hand came at her. They smelt so pungent, this close, that it was the smell rather than the (relatively gentle) prod the Giant gave her which almost knocked her over.

Now came the Giant's first speech to her in such close proximity.

The force of his breath was not too great. As he opened his

mouth, and she had to throw her head back to follow the course of his tusks (she felt she needed to keep an eye somehow most of all on these incisors) what was also almost a knock-out was the heady enveloping pungent fragrance of his breath. For it was a fragrance: a very big, dark fragrance of blood, of inside flesh, that he had last eaten, also his own. The bacteria living in a Giant's mouth are no bigger than other bacteria but there are more of them. Nevertheless, they were healthy bacteria. The Giant was a healthy, happy carnivore. Julia, of course, thought of him as a Beast, since she had been brought up in a civilised manner.

'Are you good to eat?' the Giant asked.

'No,' Julia said.

That exchange seemed to be over.

But no, alas, here was a cannibal.

'Why were you travelling with the eagle?' the Giant asked simply. 'These engines run on the highest quality fuel, you know. If the eagle was going to use you, you have plenty of juice in you.'

'Then get it over with,' Julia said.

A look of surprise entered the Giant's black gaze. But before he could take her at her word and *then* maybe reflect on her strangeness, his brothers all came in.

They deployed themselves around the cavern, populating the shadows. Sulphur whirled in eddies displaced around them. They wore fur hats made of shaggy animals – one even wore a walrus, for the icy seas were not far from here if you followed the sulphur tunnels in giant strides.

'What have you here?' the giants asked as they fletched their arrows and put their feet up.

'A good engine,' said the original ogre (Julia decided, with a flash of hostility, that you called it an ogre if it had tusks and two pairs of arms).

'And rich fuel it was storing to tank up on,' said one ogre, 'I see.' And he picked Julia from her flat palm plateau.

She was upside down suddenly, she was joggled, it was a violent sensation, she screamed '*Will* you put me down!'

The ogre put her down obediently. The first ogre said with a glimmer of impatience, 'Give it back to me.' He took storage of Julia again, this time making a fist around her, so that she was enclosed in his fingers securely.

'It makes good seasoning,' said a brother, 'and we've run out of salt.'

'Two mouthfuls and then we'd have run out of seasoning again,' said the ogre with her in his fist.

'We should have a seasoning-battery,' said an ogre. 'I've said so again and again. We get several of these high octane little treats, breed them in battery cages, and maybe we even have enough left over to sell.'

The giant with the most horrible eyebrows pinched Julia. She now knew for sure what she was in for. When giants, ogres or witches pinch you the question mark 'toothsome?' is in their minds. Almost immediately a 'morsel' was popped into Julia's mouth, or more exactly her face, by sheer pressure mostly crammed into her mouth. What was it? What had it been? It tasted stale and meaty and was probably a left-over of mutton fat. Whatever it was, she had succeeded in swallowing it before she could be sure *what* it might be – the pressure of the Horrible Giant's fingers was so great that she couldn't possibly spit it out.

Another huge glob was about to follow. Julia quickly doubled up and began deliberately retching. The Giant whose hand still held her, poked her – perhaps fairly gently though the touch left her crowing for breath, to tell her to straighten up: with another hand he halted the Horrible Eyebrows Giant's 'fattening morsel' onslaught. Julia thought she caught in her captor's eye a certain awareness, an appraising alertness.

Of course, her captor did permit her to eat. He stood her on the table in front of his glass at mealtimes. She had to lift his glass towards his hand (he indicated this by a peremptory tap of his thumb on the table, and when she looked upwards into his face for a further clue to his demand she saw a ferocious glance with, she guessed, a dangerous amusement). After a while he wanted her to lift the glass direct to his lips, huge but not immediately obvious in his scrubland of russet moustache. She could handle the glass as long as it was not full to its brim. Once she spilled it and then she found herself the other side of the table surface, amongst another giant's crude cutlery. The Horrible Giant (she just caught a glimpse of the matted cliff of white eyebrows) reached a hand to smash her (she fell under the advancing shadow) but a brother giant smote that hand away and picked her up respectfully as someone else's property and handed her back to her master.

The caves were lit by a constant pulsing sulphurous glow. The Giants were craftsmen and they made machines. They caused or augmented a banging and hammering and vibration in the rifts in the dark earth. They utilised the dark earth. Probably they were Taurus. They utilised the sulphur and fumes of the dark. Fire magnificently challenged them. Then they used it.

The Giant had a use for Julia. It was not a sexual use. He meant to be amused by her, while he fed her. Then to eat her. Julia saw how they used protein (sheep and lambs they fattened in a cave that sprouted fungus for grazing). The sheep and lambs failed to amuse. The Giants tore the lambs into shreds. They sprinkled the shreds on their main meals, which were great mounds usually of vegetables also grown in the caverns. They did not have enough protein, or large enough units of protein, to use as a main meal ever. So, they used protein as a condiment, a salt and pepper. They had genteel condiment sprinklers which they had wrought from heavy glass with curly zircon tops.

But the place in which the Giant carried Julia was the pouch on his great leathern many-buckled belt. Julia stood on the shifting floor of the loose change in the pouch while she leaned on the rim of the pouch and looked out on the world. She watched while the Giant made the parts of the great engines he and his brothers built for eventual conquering of the world. She watched while the shadows and lights ran green and orange and choking in the earth's rifts. The Giant tucked her deeper in the pouch now and then for her safety when she had been standing on tiptoe on his florins and sovereigns and forgetting her vertigo. When he went to the inner lavatorial pits to piss he pulled out his member right beneath and beside her. She thus became, although dreadfully shocked and put out at first sight of it, most familiar with its structure, the ivory ribs and columns, the spectacular veins which jumped out and throbbed occasionally blue and bright enough to light her way momentarily had she wanted to climb out along it, the low copse of ginger metallically shining wire from which it sprang once loosed on the world, the glistening beads of sweat in the tangled wire, the fragrance of it, the arc of gold and silver water it created far out into the darkness.

She became familiar with its working order, and of course the Giant was aware that she was becoming so.

Accordingly, it displayed its functionary efficiency in greater versatility. It changed shape at times. Its geometries metamorphosed. It grew. It became even longer. It thickened and stood. It was a stupendous working machine in itself.

Sometimes when it engorged and wavered, stood half up, hesitated and half fell, then miraculously lifted itself up by its very bootstraps and stood high, the Giant would not put it away. He would play the fingers of one or two of his left hands along it. He would strum it with a subtle ease. His fingers would work in a rhythm Julia would grow used to (for even if she sneered and went down into the depths of his money-purse and declined to look, the rhythm would continue to shake her). Then the rhythm would change. It would become lazy but less subtle, more obvious. Then it would change again, to a smooth rapid rage. At this time, she would feel the Giant's body behind her, taut and magnetic (she was almost irresistibly pulled towards that side of the purse, as by electric current). All the normal working rhythms in the giant's body would magnify and race. She would be in the midst of a fairly audible tumult, as of some termite city that is under perfect control and swiftens its pace without panic. Sometimes she would clamber up to see what was happening now at any rate. A mighty pulsation as of an engine completing some urgent working cycle would shake her. The Giant would have both his left hands, maybe one of his right hands, going back and forth so savagely on the member close to her 'resting' place that all was blurred. Then a jet of cream would issue in such munificence as if a whole dairy had imploded. Once when she went up to look the Giant noted her with a gleam as the sulphur light here flared an instant, and he turned the cream upon her. She struggled back in an enveloping viscous wave which closed her eyes and nostrils. A giant digit smeared more over her. There was an undeniably wonderful all-pervasive smell. She managed to peer up at him and saw him gazing proprietorially down at her while he smeared the magic liquid over her, in her hair, down her neck, up her dress, and the giant member dangled humpish and ivory beside her. When she was back in the communal workshop the stuff hardened upon her – like a helmet upon her hair, like cracked nougat on her dress. He laughed when he plucked her out in the evening: and unhardened the stuff by playing a musical jet of urine upon her, for washing water was in short supply and neither she nor he were due any till the next day, and anyway having Mercury in Taurus in their composite horoscope chart it appeared that Julia and her captor communicated with each other through the medium of excreta of one kind or another.

As he grew bolder with her (he had been more awkward at first) he communicated more warmly, sending her on the trek round to his rear passage with big sheets of toilet paper (which to her were more like sizings of hardboard) and he would fart while she cleaned him (she perched like a window cleaner in a kind of steeplejack harness of bits of his belt, which was vastly complicated since from its straps and buckles were suspended his comb, spanners, such tools). His farts also were communication, gentle and warm, very soft-pedalled so as not to throw her off her cradle and, she thought, affectionate: from her days as a smaller child rolling in the great playground of the Castle stables, she thought she remembered some of the great stallions doing much the same thing as a kind of mark of appreciation while you groomed them. When he played with himself which was more regularly now as though he took it to be a pact understood, he would make her stand up against the member (it was when grown about the size of herself) and roll the great ivory grey and blue foreskin vertically back and forward at the full stretch of both her arms. This necessarily caused her to rub herself up and down against it too, and the warm trembling which gradually seized her was, she realised, a very vivid and addictive exercise. A finger and the thumb of one or two of his hands would take time to flick out and rub her in turn. She was, she realised, having a sexual relationship. She just thought it was a shame that he was going to eat her and they could never get to know each other on a more cerebral level. It was possible, it is true, for the Giant to speak to her but even when in his bed at night he took her out and placed her on his straw-filled pillow beside his head, and turned and fixed her squinting with his glittering eye, and talked, she was always (a) uncomfortably aware of his huge tongue and teeth, (b) nearly blown across the pillow by the blast of his breath, occasionally she did think of recommending a decent toothpaste, and

(c) she was unable to make out much of the content of what he said, for it was mostly a thunder and a rumble.

' . . . rumble mumble ahhh shsh haah . . . ' he would say, all his vowels shaking her and his consonants either detonating or hissing, and then she would catch three words about difficult schematic fans and multi-stage compressors, or two phrases about the meaning of life and the penalties of Mercury rising.

She would lean and look up at him, or which bits of him she could best ascertain, and she understood his mood and his meanings in some way which were not to do with her ignorance of his words.

Then he might pause, and aspirate gaspingly almost sucking her in to that tooth-fringed bristling-fringed depth which she considered her probable eventual fate, and lean down towards her politely and expectantly for her answer.

She might reach up to his ear, grab hold of the lobe and shout into the whorling drum, which hit her with echoes back. 'I DIDERNT QUITE CATCH QUITE ALL YOU WERE DISCOURSING ON BUT I REALLY AGREE ABOUT MERCUREE I THINK,' and he would shake his head suddenly and slap at his eardrum (narrowly missing her) as though a gnat had blown into it, and shake his head again and look at her frustrated. He talked a lot, which she liked though she didn't understand it, but when he fell asleep he snored like an alien thing altogether, a volcano or something similarly and ominously topographical, and she rolled away from him and lay hanging on to the pillow. She dare not climb down into the cave, for rats ran and scavenged and fought down there on the floor while the giant slept, so sometimes she would climb into his curls and pull them round her for warmth, but when he woke up and sat up suddenly (which shot her up very high in the world) and ran his fingers roughly through his hair she realised her mistake. Sometimes she scrambled down and curled in the curve of his neck and shoulder, which she liked, but if he moved suddenly that was dangerous and she could be crackerjacked without his ever knowing till perhaps he found her broken and thought 'Shame – waste' – so she discovered the best place, and warm too, was down in his ringlety crotch hanging on with both arms round her friend the great member, as in the Castle she had held a one-eyed teddy bear at night, with her cheek against its fragrant living satin. If he woke and put a hand down to scratch there or shift himself lovingly, he did so tenderly and felt her and seemed pleased she was there and would lift her lightly and let her drop again in a sweet way and soon this was usually the start of a morning session. She could be useful in other ways too she found – the giants' needles were large but light, since they were only bone hollowed to slit and thread, and she could control the thread, which being only ordinary sheep-gut she could knot and re-knot more easily than could giant fingers. She sewed up rents in his giant twill shirts, but when other giants wanted her to patch their garments she refused: she shook her whole self rather than just her head, for they seemed to find her usual bodily gestures too delicate for understanding. Her own Giant upheld her, and would not make her work for anyone else. She cleaned his great shoes and was very thorough. She scrambled over him in his once-weekly tub of boiled sulphur-scummed water; she soaped his ringlets, which made her feel as though she wallowed in the lushest of surf. She made herself, as well as he, wonderfully clean. The few lice or similar parasites which had gambolled in those pastures now were banished. She, instead, played.

But however clean she became she wondered, as she sat conscientiously polishing his uppers, and scraping his laces, and buffing his toecaps of reinforced and now weatherproofed canvas, whether she had become debauched. And she decided that perhaps she hadn't, since when you looked at it fairly from one sane and logical direction at least, she was still quite intact and likely in this situation to remain so until she was eaten. And this is an intrinsically crucial element of a relationship for a Virgoan. If their relationship is heavy traffic, they contrive to retain an element of their self, whether it be their bodily self, as now in Julia's case, or some other aspect of the self. She felt she would rather like to say to her free-flying friend Peir, as (it might be) he dropped in while she was rolling in her mighty host's ringlets, or carousing in his crotch, that she had loosened up pretty well as Virgos go. But she could only too well imagine him languidly sneering his reply, 'You are still about as relaxed as a new tap-washer, Julia, and you will always be more Crawling than Mutable.'

Julia by now, of course, knew that her brother Cabel must be either alive or dead. It is a predicament in which anyone absent from anyone else finds themselves. Indeed, unless one can keep one's dearests extremely near the entire while, one is constantly to be unaware as to whether at this precise instant they happen to be alive.

Julia was glad that she was to be eaten.

It made her feel better, sharpened her up, during chores and carousals which otherwise would have made her feel soggy (in psyche, you understand) and blurred.

It would have felt unbearably poignant and unfaithful to engage in these bizarre orgasms – but for the fact that even though her darling little brother was gone, she too would soon be gone. That eased the horror, softened it, made life seem the stranger, death the familiar, death the family.

And just buffing the Giant's shoes or sewing on his immense crude buttons took on a certain stern poetry when it was a task she might rarely perform again: by the time this button next popped off, she would not be there to sew it again, so it was really worth sewing it well. And when something is worth doing, it's much less debilitating to have to get on with it.

Thus, because every day here might be her last, Julia got through each tolerably well and soon, in constant expectation of termination, discovered that she had been here a season.

What season had it been when she was deposited by the wicked, justly punished bird in this rift in the ground? It had to all outward signs, intents and purposes been summer. Now, when she peeped up at the world, which occasionally from certain periscopal points was possible, she saw that all was mists and rainbows up there. The sun shone still, but on shifting airs, on winds and changing pigments, making itself into prisms.

The world indeed was refusing to stand still, refusing to stand firm. The world was moving on without her; the world was faithless, as she had been to Cabel.

It made her itch to get up there again, to catch the world and not be left behind at the stop.

And now what a dilemma. She had been becalmed by false promises of death. Annihilation had been her destination for so long, that she felt bereft without it. She had travelled on past it and now where was she? It had been her prop. Now the roof might fall on her after all – what was there to stop it? What was she supposed to do if she went up there into the world? She couldn't search for Cabel – too long had elapsed for there to be a clue.

A bit upsetting, that. She'd sooner go on dying safely down here.

The relationship with the Giant was reaching new heights and depths. Or rather, the relationship with his member. For a relationship with him was really rather beyond her. They knew a bit about each other, but it was all in the present tense. They really were unable to exchange pasts, unable to reminisce much.

But the understanding between Julia and his outpost was becoming quite a rapport. The member was her friend, her master, her slave. She felt she might really miss it if she left now. Still, this situation was a bit of a cul-de-sac. The art of conversation between the Giant and Julia was not burgeoning, though between Julia and his member it was flowering into a renaissance, a true Golden Age. She threw her arms around it in its sleep and nuzzled it at the thought that she might soon be gone, and although asleep it rose a little and its hump throbbed in her direction responsively, physically.

She left a note for the Giant. She wrote as huge as she could, on one of his sheets of toilet paper (their communication was Mercury in Taurus to the last) with a stub of charcoal from one of the carbon and silica furnace caverns.

'THANK YOU FOR YOUR HOSPITALITY. WE KNOW NOTHING ABOUT EACH OTHERS LITTLE LIKES AND DISLIKES. PERHAPS I AM ONE OF YOUR LITTLE LIKES. I HOPE SO. I WILL NEVER BE ABLE TO THANK YOU ENOUGH FOR NOT EATING ME.'

She paused, signed – 'JULIA, THATS MY NAME', and crept out to one of the periscope points, where, since the Giant began increasingly to trust her, she had been able to rig up a sort of rope ladder secretly, woven away from his once-strict surveillance out of discarded sweepings from the workfloors.

There were no rats in the Giant's room nowadays, for she had made it all so neat and tidied away left-overs. And when he'd found her laboriously dragging a firewood log in front of a rat-hole, he'd put boulders in front of them all for her.

She climbed up her rope ladder. The Giant lay sleeping. As she mounted higher into his ceiling, he fell into perspective behind her and began to look less like a collection of too closely observed angles and characteristics: 'thus,' she thought, 'most relationships look after you leave them.' She hung there for a moment gazing backwards: he could be seen now all in one piece, and was visible as a young man, with two pairs of arms each side and obtrusive although handsome tusks, a look of brooding contentment on his face, a certain melancholy pride in the set of his brows and mouth, a certain individuality and aloneness in his jaw and the set of his shoulders, which she had never before been in a position to judge. As she paused there, gazing as it were for the first time at his nakedness (for the coarse coverlet had fallen back) she saw his member give a great jump and it startled her into a reminder of her situation. She regained her balance and hurried on up the 'ladder' towards the stars. Not a moment too soon: for as she stepped out on to the crater under the moon, the Giant awoke and reached his hand down to his groin for her. Peering down, she saw him look puzzled: he sat up on the bed, all his hands groping around in different directions for her. There was a shout from him, then, which shook the earth on which she stood. She stopped peering down, for with these vibrations she was in danger of falling back whence she'd climbed. She hastened (the earth was barren here and only she awake, it seemed, under the moon) to the hills which she knew meant Forest. She kept to cover all the way (there were boulders and stumps) and this was wise for presently she heard pursuit behind her. The Giants, dressed in their vulcanised rubbers and canvases, had hurried up on to the plateau and were beating around with sticks and shouting. She reached the Forest well before them (strange that the Forest now should seem a refuge to her) and inched herself lithely in among its soft humming glades. She climbed a tall tree. She heard the Giants pause and stop at the outskirts of the Forest. They did not enter. That was not their terrain. They could not breathe in this element. They needed fire and sulphur and earth, they were earth, like Antaeus they would weaken into wraiths if they left their element. She slept in the tall tree beside a sleeping violet coloured parrot. She wondered throughout her dreams if the Giant's violet coloured cock had jumped and woken the Giant in order to alert him to pursue her, or in order to warn *her* to hasten on to her escape at long last.

The Last of His Breed

Rob Chilson

'No horse ever born could take that slope at that speed and live,' mused Ken Hastie, looking down it. Parts of Arizona are quite rugged, and this was one of them. He was looking down a mountainside. The slope was by no means a cliff, but he would have walked his horse down it even in his wildest youth. The tracks he'd been following approached it well spaced, obviously at a good fast lope if no real gallop.

Dismounting, Hastie kicked at a fairly fresh horseball. This morning, near dawn, he thought. There was no dead or wounded horse at the foot of the slope.

There were not even any tracks on the slope.

Leading his horse, his picked his way down it. The horse, a sturdy brown with plenty of sense in his think-tank, was no longer young either, and had come far since before sun-up; it gave him no trouble, allowing him to concentrate on the slope.

Near the bottom he found fragments of two more horseballs, widely spaced. Both were fragmented as if they had fallen some distance. There were no tracks, horse or animal, anywhere near either of them.

Hastie rolled himself a cigarette, musing. His eye tended to climb; he kept tracing the scarps and slopes above him, always swinging out into the pale keen blue of the stainless sky. Every wheeling bird-dot took his instant attention.

When he had smoked half his cigarette he said, 'Well.' Not a talkative man, Hastie had no words for the feelings he was experiencing, but that was not new to him. He blew smoke four ways, which the horse might have noted had it been as profound a student of human nature as he was of horse nature. But this time the act didn't signify the end of a train of thought.

Still, Hastie mounted as if this show was over. The brown carried him off along the slopes. Their day's work wasn't half done, and Hastie and the horse went about it with professional economy: eyeing the stock for fitness and flesh, discovering its locations, checking the pasturage, examining every spring and stream they passed. Hastie was not to be distracted, but not infrequently he looked aloft, and no bird passed but that his eye noted.

It was dusk when they came down, tired horse and tired man, onto the gentle series of terraces above the ranch. By the smell the ranch hands had been cutting hay; it grew lushly in these irrigated bottoms, and the smell of cows was thick. Hastie scorned to look at these fat, short-horned animals, much less to drop his rope on one.

The ranch hands were congregated on the porch of the Number Two bunkhouse. They laughed and talked in an island in the darkness, slapping mosquitos. Hastie turned the brown loose, spread his saddle blanket, draped the saddle over the rail, there being no rain in prospect. He moved mechanically.

Though his hair was getting a little grizzled before the ears, he was by no means old; it wasn't physical weariness that tied him down. Nor hunger. He had arisen before dawn, before the cooks, and ridden off without breakfast. Cowboys scorned to carry food like damned picnickers, and he'd returned after the fires were out and the remainders thrown to the hogs. But that was usual, and he didn't even notice it.

Passing the ranch hands with a nod, he entered the darkened bunkhouse and sought his bunk. Stretching out on it, hands behind his head, he continued the day's musings. No one noticed anything unusual; it wasn't usual for him to join the evening talk. What could a cowboy talk about with ranch hands?

The foreman's name was Tim Conroy and he was a good man with cows and knew it and wouldn't tolerate a hand who wasn't also pretty damn good. No one on the R Bar A mishandled a cow; even profanity was frowned on unless it sounded cheerful. The steers' negligible minds mustn't be disturbed; they must concentrate on putting on weight – good, solid, marbled beef. And no prima donnas, either – among the hands. When work was to be done they all dived in and did it. Conroy pitched in right along with the hands, as he bluntly told them. And did more work than any, which he didn't need to tell them.

One of his work-hardened hands rested now on the rail of the boss's house's porch. His round red face earnest, looking not unlike one of his own short-horns, he looked up into the equally full-fed features of Carmichael, the manager. The Roy and Andy of the brand and name were gone; the R Bar A was owned by a New York bank.

'It's the cowboy, boss. This makes the second time. Now, yestiddy, he was up in the hills, tending to his stock. That's all right. But day before, now. What was he doin' then? Shoeing horses, I could understand, but all he did was mess around the smithy. And this mornin' he went there again. Now, boss, we *got* to git that hay in.'

Carmichael had given up trying to keep the men from calling him boss. He looked into the distance, reckoning the R Bar A's fields and the number of hands.

'If it's that bad, I can find a couple of part-timers in the Springs till the season's over.'

'I hate pick-up and drop-off labour,' said Tim. 'The cowboy's a good steady dependable man. No reason to my notion why he can't pitch hay.'

Banging sounds came from the smithy. 'Goddamn!' said Conroy.

'Well, I can tell you one thing.' Carmichael idly kicked a porch post. 'He didn't help you fix fence day before yesterday, not because he was so busy, but because he damn well wouldn't.'

'What?'

'Fact. 'Fore you come, him and one of those pepper-eatin' cow-ponies of his busted down the corral fence, which is rails and not even wire, and he wouldn't help fix it. Left it to us.'

'Goddamn! When he broke it down hisself? And you stood for that?'

Carmichael smiled, half-wry, half-admiring. 'Tim, there's near three thousand head of longhorn stock up in the hills. They'll run twenty, twenty-five per cent of the ranch's income, end of the year. And there ain't but one man of us knows how to take care of 'em. Could you do it if he was to quit? Could any of the hands?'

Tim shook his head, but frowned and said, 'But –' He stopped, started again. 'You're sayin' that even if *you* ordered him –'

'He calls me boss same as the rest of you, but I don't tell him to do nothing he don't want to do. I'm not givin' him orders to pitch hay.'

Hastie crossed a distant yard between the smithy and the stable.

Tim's temper flared. 'Goddamn! Look at him! Walks like he owns the earth.'

'No,' mused Carmichael. 'That's a different kind of freedom. More like he doesn't need the earth. Think of a horse with wings.'

Ken Hastie spent the entire summer preparing for winter. He checked his ropes and replaced any that wouldn't take the strain. He patched his waterproof. He made sure every strap of both saddles was tightly anchored, of the strongest leather. He soaped and rubbed endlessly. From spurs to wooden buckets to hat nothing escape his eye, and his boots he replaced every autumn when he could afford to.

And every third or fourth day he checked on his stock.

Last year there had been a wild cat. He'd sold the hide in Excelsior Springs. This year nothing . . . nothing he could tell of. Now he overhauled his stoutest saddle and considered another visit to the range. Not to check on the stock. To look for a horse. . .

The scrunch of feet on gravel caused him to look up. Carmichael, the boss, or at least the bosses' representative, approached him, dressed in his dark coat. Beyond, the plum-coloured Packard was backed up to the porch. Going to town.

'A week ago you said the situation for horses in the hills isn't so good this year.' Carmichael began without preliminary – the best way to deal with the cowboy.

'Yeah, they're gettin' wild, and besides, the cattle're eatin'em off the range.'

'And you're not too well fixed for horses?'

Hastie thumbed his hat back, straightening up, automatically looked at the sky. 'I was just thinkin' about that. Want to go back up and scout for horses, but I don't hold out much hope – and if I have to spend a month catchin'em, I won't have time to break'em. Course, I don't need cow-ponies for this winter, just good strong willin' horses.'

'Strong, young, and willing. Care to come along to pick'em out?'

Hastie looked at the Packard. It had sixteen cylinders, they said, but he was only vaguely aware of what a cylinder was, and it looked the same as another car that only had twelve. It was fast, but not his kind of fast. Suppose it got the bit in its teeth, how could anyone ever hold it in?

'I got enough to do to keep me busy a week. Besides, you're a tolerable judge of horseflesh.'

'Okay, I'll do my best. Anything else you need?'

Hastie shook his head, returning to his work.

Carmichael stood watching him a moment. But this was the man who left Texas because they wanted him to fix fence. He'd sworn never to return, and Carmichael, to whom he'd told that, didn't for a moment doubt he'd keep his word.

'Okay, I'll see what they got.'

Hastie tugged on a string, unaware of the crisis that had passed.

Hastie took food with him the next day and two horses, and was gone before sun-up. Nobody but Tim Conroy missed him.

'What a hell of a thing! And we got to have him,' he said to his strawboss, Linwood by name. 'The boss says it'd take the whole crew near a month to bring the wild stock down from the hills, but that ride-ever'where cowboy can do it in less'n a week, even in a blizzard.'

'Catch me up in them hills in a blizzard,' said Linwood contemplatively, shaking his head.

'We'd lose half the crew off the cliffs,' Conroy said, glum. 'What makes a man too good to pitch hay? Or manure? Hell, he ain't no better'n you or me!'

'Not as good, to my notion,' said Linwood, and spat. 'A man that won't work ain't in *my* class.'

But Conroy was fair-minded. 'Oh, he works, right enough. But only at what he wants to. Prima donna!'

'He's a lightweight. Mark my words, someday he's gonna fly off and leave us.'

Hastie spent two days looking at horse tracks. He was mindful of the duty he owed his employer and looked at every cow and every stream and every bit of grass that he came across, and, spending hours scanning the mountainsides, took automatic note of distant pastures. But his mind was on none of this.

'A loner.'

High up, higher than stock normally went, he found its tracks. By now he knew them as well as a face. A bit of meadow-land on a high shoulder, the snow-breath air cool in high summer. The strange horse had grazed here alone for parts of three days. The tracks and 'sign' – droppings – indicated it had been here on three successive days, but it hadn't eaten enough to feed that size of horse for three days.

Ergo, it came and went.

Hastie had seen no tracks coming or going. He looked at the sky, saw nothing. At other places he'd seen its tracks mingled with that of a few head of wild horses still pasturing here. They didn't seem to avoid it, but of course couldn't follow it.

The next day he saw it.

A distant dark shape on a mountainside. He brought it to middle distance with his binoculars, studied it as carefully as he could.

It looked like a normal horse at this distance, with these lenses, but very deep in the chest. Broad-shouldered, too, he thought. Sleek, its sides shining, not quite the *texture* of the back and neck. Dark brown with a hint of flame, near as he could make out through the chromatic aberration.

It had been grazing and gazing about in a desultory fashion, and aware of its habits as he was, he was not surprised when it began to run across the mountainside. Turning sharply down the slope, it spread its wings and was airborne.

Hastie watched it glide out, tilt sidewise in a falling turn, and start around the mountain it'd been on. Then the great wings came down and it surged forward and up in the air, its legs folded, its head high, nostrils expanded – he couldn't see that fine detail, and it was turning its back – but Hastie knew horses.

Did a distant, joyous neigh come back?

It was gone. Hastie lowered the glasses, still staring after it, with no words for his feelings. He could only repeat: 'Always alone. Prob'ly the last of its kind.'

A man doesn't have wings, and, having none, has responsibilities. They paid Hastie to do a job.

'I'm shiftin' the stock to the south, boss. There's good pasturage there.'

'All right. – I thought you said the present pasture would be adequate for awhile yet?'

'It's not in bad shape, but I want the stock on good ground before I leave.'

Carmichael looked up, startled. 'Leave!' He stood up from the rocking chair, looked down at Hastie beside the porch. 'You're going to – why? Did Tim tell you to pitch hay, or something? 'Cause that isn't your job –'

'No, no. I got no complaints, boss, but I been here nigh on to three years now. Time I curled my tail and drifted.'

'But. My God, Hastie, you can't just up and leave us. You know two years ago I couldn't find a cowboy to take your place –'

That was the occasion when Hastie had told him why he'd left Texas – he'd quit this job then. Carmichael had kept him on till he could find a replacement, which he never did.

'I been thinkin' about that. I'll put the stock where they'll be all right for three weeks, a month or five weeks if it rains. You can find someone.'

Carmichael shook his head, flung out his hands helplessly.

'If you can't find anybody, you might try that fellow Slim works at the livery in town. He's a fair hand with horses and I seen him rope.'

'You said two years ago he'd never be a cowboy.'

'No, he won't, but he's the best around.'

Hastie's real objection to Slim was that the young man had once taken a job on a ranch where he had milked cows.

Hastie himself had once owned a small ranch. He'd taken up land, cut logs, built a tiny cabin and a larger stable, a corral, outbuildings, and fixed his own fences and milked his own cow, as well as feeding slops to a pig he had kept one summer. But a man, even a cowboy, will do for himself what he won't for others, for pay. Slim would never be a cowboy.

Moving the stock was a tedious but not difficult operation. Hastie had brought them down from the mountains in the teeth of a blizzard once, and had fought through more ordinary snow-storms to bring out stock that had been missed in the earlier sweeps, bucking through waist-deep snow. Those terrible struggles against great odds were not to him romantic or thrilling.

His was a flat, matter-of-fact outlook. Hard work and danger were a part of the way of life of a cowboy. Romance was for women-folks, reading books.

He just called it a job. Tim Conroy would have approved.

It was that attitude that held Hastie motionless now.

He sat his horse with its feet on gravel, drinking from a clear mountain stream. The stream bank was just before him, about the height of his knees. Along it grew a screening line of willow and aspen. Beyond the screen was a rather brushy glade.

The horse with wings was there.

It had ignored his unsuspecting approach, hearing nothing unusual in a horse's advance to the stream for a drink; the breeze was up the mountain, from it to him. It spread its left wing now and licked the underside, oblivious.

Hastie's rope was just in front of his hand, and the horse's neck was within easy reach of a throw. He'd seen it in motion once before, on the ground, and knew that it had to have considerable speed to get into the air, like one of those aeroplanes Hastie had heard of. It would be a savage battle, with the horse leaping and beating its powerful wings, but he could have had it.

But he'd made a man a promise.

Besides, he'd sort of made himself a promise.

And what's more, he owed it to the horse, didn't he?

The horse spread its wings, stretching, and flapped them silently a couple of times. Wind blew out from it. It was a fairly large horse, dark brown with a red cast to its hair, a hint of subdued fire where the sun ran along it. The wings weren't covered with feathers as he'd thought, but with what looked like shingles of horsehair. Hastie had never heard of agglutinated hair and thought a rhino's horn was made of horn, but he compared the shingles to horsehair licked into place and sticking together wet, continuing to stick after drying. Glued together.

The horse, ignoring the restless shifting of the cow-pony's feet, made a lonely whickering sound and tossed its head, looking all about it. Then it charged across the dell, spread its wings, flapped them heavily and with some noise – but not much, for its size – and again, and was airborne, folding its legs back but low yet. Circling, its wings beating easily, it climbed until it found the uprush of air along the mountainside, and wheeled into the sky.

'It wouldn't 'a' been right,' said Hastie to no one, looking after it without expression.

The sorrel snorted softly and stamped to dislodge a fly.

Tim Conroy was outraged. 'My God, boss, a man doesn't just up and walk off from a job because he feels like he's been there too long! Now if he had a reason, or could make more – We should 'a' fired him a long time ago.'

'I would have, if I could have found a replacement. I've come to appreciate cowboys some since, Tim, and I doubt if any replacement would've been any better. Cowboys were an independent bunch.'

Tim shook his head, unable to picture a world in which the best men were so independent they thought nothing of throwing up a good job on a whim. If his best men were like that, the ranch would fall apart. Nothing would get done.

'They're not just working men, Tim. They're highly skilled technicians, like automobile mechanics. Automobiles are fairly new, so not many people know about them, but there's a lot of 'em, so there's a great need for mechanics. It was the same for cowboys.'

'How could you run a ranch when all the hands are prima donnas?'

'I guess it cancels out. And they're good at keeping their word, taken all around.'

Tim considered all that, shook his head. A prima donna was a prima donna to his mind. 'What about Raynard? I already made it plain to him that he's no better than the rest of us. I'll have him pitchin' hay the day after he shows up. Think he'll quit? He didn't seem to take it hard.'

'Hastie said he'd never be a cowboy. I expect he's right. But he's the best I could find. Cowboys are gone . . . If Slim will pitch hay, have him pitch. I just hope to hell he can handle stock, too.'

Tim nodded soberly at that.

Carmichael shook his head. 'Like I said. He's the last of his breed.'

It would rain. Good. That'd stretch the pasturage a week, if it rained enough. Hastie sat down and slid his booted feet under his waterproof. Unbuckling his belt, he slid his pants down his legs to the boot-tops, then drew his feet out of his boots. In the old days, during round-ups, he undressed that way routinely. He had only to dive his feet down into his boots and pull up his pants to be ready to ride, in the event of an emergency, and the loose waterproof kept everything dry.

Sliding dexterously sideways into the bedroll, he lay musing, looking at the stars being cut off by the encroaching clouds.

Hastie had finished moving the stock, as he'd promised, but hadn't gone back to the ranch. It no longer held anything he wanted.

It had been a long life, though he wasn't forty yet. Cowboys were gone, and the future belonged to the ranch hands, fixing barbed wire and stall-feeding short-horns with grain. There just wasn't much place left for a man who hadn't been able to make a go of ranching on his own. To continue working, you had to be a ranch hand.

Not me, he thought.

Hastie wondered how it felt to pilot an aeroplane. He thought he knew the breed of men who did. Young, they were, and independent, and proud of themselves, their craft, and their skill . . .

His father'd been like that. Hastie was born on the open range, a birth that killed his mother. With that, the heart went out of his father, who was killed in a common dust-up at a corral branding when his horse went down.

After his father was killed, Hastie was taken in hand by a small rancher his father had befriended. The old man raised him on up to years of discretion. He'd been good at breaking horses and roping cattle before he was old enough to drink. He'd ranged the west from beyond the Canadian border to beyond the border of Old Mexico. For a time there in the south he'd ridden the high trails of outlawry, rustling cattle south of the border and bringing them north, to sell them again south of the border.

He'd associated with The Men Who Can't Come Back, that inglorious legion, at that time, and been offered the job of working a machine-gun with some of them, in the pay of a gang of ragged promoters of liberty, equality, fraternity. But he didn't speak the language, and those people didn't speak his language. Their promises, even the white men, were no good, and he wouldn't associate with someone he couldn't trust. So he'd come back, and had ridden down from the high trails, which he figured meant he was grown up now and not a wild young cowboy.

'I always thought growin' up and gettin' old were the same thing. Now I figure one causes the other. Wonder which . . .'

The brown came down out of the mountains alone. It wore no saddle, nor were there reins on its bridle. Yet its presence smelled of death. The ranch hands milled about, hushed and solemn.

'He had two horses, boss,' said Tim Conroy, subdued. 'This'n and the sorrel. One packed and the other rode.'

'Likely he and the sorrel are piled up at the bottom of some slope,' said Carmichael.

'What about Hastie?'

'We're bound to look for him. But, Tim, this crew can't handle that. We haven't all that many good riding horses, not suitable for mountain work –'

'Or men who can ride that well,' said Conroy quietly.

'Right. I'll take Raynard; we'll ride Hastie's horses – have Slim saddle the bay and the new gelding. We'll take the brown along for Hastie, it doesn't look too tired. Evidently it never panicked.'

'It was out to pasture when it happened, I reckon.'

'Yes. The two of us'll have to do – you keep the hands busy.'

'Right. And – good luck, boss.'

For days Hastie had sought a certain place he'd never seen. A cove or valley high up on a mountain, shielded from the northwest winds. It needn't be very big, nor have much pasturage.

When he found that bedding ground, he found more: the spring where the winged horse drank. Characteristically, this was not even on the same mountain; it swooped over above a narrow valley for its morning drink. Hastie spent all night getting into position; there was time only for a couple of hours of restless sleep before the pre-dawn light woke him.

He was ready, suppressing any reaction to the chill of morning, looking down on the spring. It was like a cup hacked out of a steep house roof. The wind was favourable, behind the horse on its matutinal swoop. Hastie was calm, at peace. He'd left his camp neat, the horses unhobbled, all promises filled.

And there it came, wheeling against the blue-grey sky, great wings spread wide. It grew and grew and grew. Then the wings came together, and again, and again, and Hastie's hat vibrated on his head. He slitted his eyes and didn't move. Wheeling sharply, its wing tip seeming to brush the steep scarp, it came level and folded its wings, landed springily at a trot on the nearly level spot before the break in the slope where the spring bubbled out.

It walked coolly forward, lowered its proud head, standing almost under Hastie on the rim of the cup. He'd studied its tracks well and knew where to put himself. It drank, raised its head, looked about; lowered its head again. Hastie, who'd had no breakfast, let it drink its fill. Then he sprang on its back.

It reared with an angry neigh, wheeled in the close quarters, bucked once, kicking. Hastie's legs held its wings closed, but as it erupted out of the cup he gambled, slipping first one leg up and then the other far enough to let it unfold them. The horse sprang forward, neighing again in fury, and beat its wings. Hastie's hat flew off; the string caught it. A bucking leap took them into the air. The world swooped and spun around them. Hastie gasped for breath, fear an emptiness in his belly, a grip in his legs and hands. His fingers ached in the horse's mane.

The horse made an amazing buck in mid-air, but it was nothing to Hastie, since it lacked the spine-wracking jolt at the end. It spun about abruptly, dived, beat upward, and none of these evolutions were so severe as those a horse could make, thrusting hoofs against solid ground. Only the slippery insecurity of horsehair under his pants made them dangerous. Hastie still panted, but his stark fear had eased.

Then the horse turned upside down. He felt his legs slipping, only his hands held him on, death was near – thousands of feet down – But the horse could no more tolerate that than he, and righted itself in time.

It can't fly upside down! he thought. And he knew he'd won.

The horse levelled out, sobbing for breath and fear, and looked back at him. Its eyes were white-ringed. A surge of confidence came over Hastie and he let his eyes sweep around. Mountains before and behind and to every side, slopes here, there and everywhere, valleys and canyons below. All theirs now.

The horse was over the first panicked fury, building up

strength for the next bout. Hastie leaned forward, talking softly to it. Now he was confident; he knew he could not fail. For Hastie knew horses. He could foresee each successive battle, each trick and sleight and feint, and knew that he could not lose. Each battle would leave him stronger and the horse more docile.

'There now, there now, it's not so bad, is it?'

He'd made up his mind never to tie it down, he'd brought no rope with him, nothing but hobbles and bridle. It would be the ultimate test of his skill, to tame and train this creature of the sky without breaking its spirit or letting it escape. But he felt nothing but the most unutterable confidence in his ability.

They flew easily across the sky, riding the thermals above the mountains, swooping and soaring, and his heart beat high for fear and joy. What a horse!

Abruptly it 'broke in half', kicked in mid-air, bucked, spun, flipped over on its back – that nearly caught him – and bucked again. Hastie, gasping for breath, held on with a fierce elation, knowing he could not lose, that this was his fated horse, this sky his sky.

He'd been training for this all his life . . .

Tim Conroy watched sharply to his right, and when the rake came even with the hay, he heaved down on the lever. The curved tines of the rake raised and dumped the rolling cylinder of hay they'd scraped up. The little pinto pony perked steadily on at its light trot and he dropped the tines again. The pony was smart and already knew the pattern, making now for the next line of hay. Tim held himself ready at all times to kick his heels in the air and roll backwards out of the big iron seat if bumblebees should go for the horse, lest he fall off in front and be dragged to death when the horse panicked.

At the end of the field they circled and he glanced swiftly around, saw nothing amiss, and let his eyes go to the mountains beyond. Slim and the boss were still out there, but it'd been a couple of days, and Tim knew that they'd never bring the cowboy back alive. He doubted if they'd even find the body. Fell off some cliff, likely, or went off when one of those half-wild ponies started bucking for no reason at all, as they frequently did. He shook his head morbidly. Too bad.

But there were near three thousand head of stock up there, and their care now became a part of his, Tim Conroy's responsibilities. He'd sized up young Slim Raynard and agreed with Hastie; the man'd never be a cowboy. He took orders too easily, as if he knew no better than anyone what to do.

Tim shook his head again. But for the moment it wasn't the responsibility he regretted. It was the man. *There* was a man who walked like he had wings on his back and didn't need the earth. Strange how empty that quiet man had left the ranch.

'Too bad. They don't make men like that no more.'

Tim heaved the rake's teeth up, dropped them. For a moment his gaze focused on the sunset sky. A large dark object with wings wheeled across its glory and gold. But Tim was a ranch hand, whose cows never died on distant ranges. 'Tracks in the sky' meant nothing to him. He couldn't even have said whether or not it was a bird, though he never realised that.

A much-travelled British telecommunications executive who has now turned to full-time writing and lives in Essex, Garry Kilworth is the author of several novels including *In Solitary*, *Gemini God* and the recent *A Theatre of Timesmiths*. His fantasy variation has classic haunted house overtones with a difference.

The House that Joachim Jacober built

Garry Kilworth

Caleb stopped the car and cut the lights. Immediately, he regretted the action. The darkness of deserted moorland closed round him with a frightening, soundless *snap* and he quickly switched them back on again.

'This is silly,' he said, gripping the wheel. 'I can't sit here all night with the lights blazing. The battery will be flat in a couple of hours.'

But the fact remained, he was lost and to continue driving with half a gallon of petrol in the tank was idiocy – especially on the edge of Bodmin moor. He was lost and a little afraid. It was a sad fact that at thirty-one years of age he was still scared of the dark. Turning on the motor to interrupt an eternal stillness, he drove a few more yards to the top of a rise. And there it was. A *house*. No lights on but it *was* a human habitation in this backwater of time. Prehistory was lodged on the shoulders of the wasteland. Its ghosts were ageless and probably not even human. Beasts, not men. Worse still, half-men – a semblance, a human shape, but without compassion for the traveller. Misty-brained and unreasonably brutal. Caleb shuddered.

He left the car with the interior lit – an island of light glowing reassurance. He could return to switch it off once he had woken the occupants of the house. The wooden steps to the veranda creaked beneath his feet. Suddenly he felt very tired. Why wake anyone? Why not sleep right here on the porch? The night was warm and he removed his jacket, folding it to make a pillow. At least in the morning he would be able to locate his position. The boards were comfortable beneath him. That was because he was exhausted. Fatigue will soften even stone. He slept. The car interior light was forgotten.

In the morning sun he woke late and remembered. Returning to the car he tried to start the motor and though the dashboard lights glowed there was not enough power to turn the engine. Caleb cursed the machine and remounted the veranda steps to knock on the door. There was no answer.

'Hey, anybody home?' he called. After a moment there was a faint reply. Shrugging, he tried the solid wooden door and it swung inwards, easily. He stepped inside.

'Hallo.' His voice echoed dully through unfurnished passageways and rooms. Inside, the hall smelled of fresh polish but was completely bare. Not even a floor covering of any kind.

'Anybody here?' As if in answer the door closed quietly behind him. The wind. He crossed to one of the rooms. Opening the door he saw that it, too, was empty. Was the whole house deserted? Stepping inside the room he looked round for a telephone, noticing the dark, beautiful panels that decorated the walls. Oak? His eyes travelled upwards and he saw that there was no ceiling, just red beams and a shiplap roof. Through the window, which lacked any glass, he could see a rusting vehicle, a truck of some kind, and beyond that a spinney. The truck was an old Ford, obviously a farmer's vehicle, since it was decorated with mud and pieces of straw. It looked abandoned and unserviceable.

But no telephone. Not in this room. Perhaps in one of the others? Builders often had a telephone installed once the place was weatherproof, especially in remote places. He could not remember seeing any poles, however. He began to cross the room. The door slammed shut in his face, violently.

What the hell? Ah, the open window. The draught. *What damned draught?*

Caleb reached for the handle. There was none. He tried to prise the door open with his fingernails but it held fast. In fact he could have sworn ... but why should the wood swell to his touch?

'Goddam,' he swore, becoming angry. The window. He would try the window.

There were no catches. It appeared that the windows had been fashioned to remain closed. There was no glass in them but they were of the type constructed to hold small panes and the framework was as thick and solid as jail bars. He tested his strength against them and found himself wanting. They refused to budge.

'Damnation! What the hell is this place anyway?'

'Calm. Keep calm.'

Caleb swung round quickly, alarmed. The room was still empty. He could see no openings in the walls or the door.

'Who said that? Who's there? Come on out, whoever you are.' There was no answer. Someone was playing childish tricks on him. Someone with a deep, rich voice and a warped sense of humour. He crossed the room to the door again but could get no purchase for his fingernails. Only a hairline crack proved the existence of an opening at all.

'Put your hand on the wall,' commanded the voice.

'Get lost,' said Caleb, his eyes searching the room for the speaker once more.

'Feel the floor then.'

Beneath Caleb's feet the floorboards began to vibrate until he found it difficult to maintain his balance. He began to experience real fear and finally fell onto his hands and knees. Still the floor continued to shake until it rattled the teeth in his mouth and the boards began to shriek at a frequency which hurt his ears.

'Stop it! Stop it! Stop it!' he screamed.

Abruptly, the motion and the noise ceased.

'I can control my communication with you to any pitch. Put your hand on the panels.'

This time Caleb did as he was told and he could feel the gentle vibration.

'You have your hand on my vocal cords,' said the house.

Caleb's mind was in a turmoil. 'Mad. I'm going mad,' he cried. 'Let me out of this place. You have no right . . .'

The house rustled a sigh. 'Madness. The human answer to all problems. Call yourself deranged if you wish. It matters little to me. You are to remain here. I need you. Hide behind your madness if you wish.'

Caleb, conscious that he was speaking to thin air but anxious to uncover any clue to the source of his recent insanity, then asked the eternal question: *why?*

The explanation was immediately forthcoming. The house

told him that it was, like Caleb, a live creature: that it was a Narcissistic being which required constant attention. Since it had no limbs to care for itself, it needed a slave. Caleb was to be that slave. He was to polish the wood until it gleamed. He was to repair and maintain the house according to the wishes of that creature. The house did not consider vanity a sin: pride in appearance was an essential ingredient of its character.

Thus Caleb learned his role in the scheme of things as envisaged by his new master. It was to be a partnership, according to the house, though Caleb could see little advantage in the arrangement for himself. He could, however, see what he had to offer the house – his *hands*. Hands with which to saw wood and fit joints. Hands with which to polish and clean the floors and walls. Hands to care for the beauty of his master. (Hands which would aid his escape as soon as he saw his chance ...)

After the lecture the house informed Caleb that it was going to allow him to leave the room. He was instructed to enter the hall and look inside a stairwell cupboard. There he would find a rope which he was to carry back inside the room.

The door swung open. Caleb entered the hall cautiously. There was no exit unbarred to him. Thick doors blocked either end of the hallway. There was a wide staircase curving up and round above his head in a majestic sweep, but he had no wish to inspect the floor above. He had no doubt that the bedrooms would be just as escape proof as the rooms on the ground floor. The tall, narrow windows of the hall and staircase were similar to the ones he had left behind him. He extracted the rope from the cupboard and re-entered the room.

He was then commanded to tie one end to a beam positioned about seven feet above the floor. He did as he was told. The beam was loose in its sockets and was greased at its ends. He was then instructed to tie the other end of the rope around his neck.

'Like hell,' said Caleb, suddenly realising the intention behind the commands.

'Go out onto the front porch. Stand on the veranda. I wish to show you something.'

Caleb passed suspiciously through the open doorways until he stood on the veranda. The way was open for him to bolt but he was curious as to the next action the house was about to take.

There followed the sound of wood under immense pressure: a straining of timbers that screamed at the sky for release. Suddenly, one of the porch posts gave with a crack like a cannon shot and a huge spar went flashing through the air to punch a hole in Caleb's car door, burying itself like a javelin in the metal. Above him, the porch sagged.

Caleb knew then that the house could kill him before he got ten yards. Even supposing it were not that accurate it could probably send a spray of slivers, like grapeshot, and cut him to pieces. He looked up at the sky: it was a heavy day with thick cloud and it matched his own morose feelings. He was a prisoner. Freedom, something he had always taken for granted, had been taken from him in a single night. It could have been anybody, but it was him. Mentally he cursed the circumstances that had led him into this unwanted position.

'Your first job will be to repair the porch,' said the house, matter-of-factly.

Caleb went back into the room and reluctantly tied the rope around his neck. It was an humiliating experience. Demeaning. His feelings almost choked him as he set about the task of repairing the broken porch post but there was simply no choice. If he was to survive he would have to do as he was told and await his chance to escape.

The house was not completely satisfied with the result of Caleb's labours but since he was not a carpenter it was to be expected that the job would be less than professional. He would have to learn, said the house. Caleb worked long hours, and hard, at first with the minimum of satisfaction. He could not help admiring the workmanship that had gone into the building of the house though. The place had been fashioned by loving hands, that was obvious. In the rooms on the second floor the panels had been carved: decorated with centripetals in their corners and in the centre of each panel, the representation of some natural shape – a sheaf of corn on one, an oak leaf on another.

Most of the rooms were plain, it was true, but there is something about the feel of wood which brings on a sense of nostalgia in people, and Caleb was no exception. He found he was touching the house, constantly, running his hand over a rail or down a pillar, just for the sensation it aroused within him.

Sensual, that was the word, though he would never have used it aloud.

The house moved incessantly. Mostly, it was just a gentle vibration but occasionally it creaked like a whale and reminded Caleb that it was a beast and not a dumb, inanimate object. Sometimes it felt inclined to talk to him and did so in those same deep tones that Caleb had heard on first entering its portals.

Caleb spent some of his resting hours among the trees, lying in their shade and watching the clouds float over them. From his vantage point in the spinney, Caleb was able to study the exterior of the house, his master. It was a two-storey building made almost completely of wood. In design it resembled a New England farmhouse, such as the type painted by the American artist, Hopper. There were no windows at the back of the house, but the three other walls shared eight between them. The porch and veranda also skirted three walls, making an open square. Nothing was painted – the bare wood was polished overall with beeswax. There was a single stone chimney standing proud at the end of the east wall.

Caleb found that the house was well stocked with provisions and there were adequate tools to work with. He was told that he was not the first: another had been before him, the man that had built the house. When asked how the house came to be a live, sentient being, the house became a little vague. It appeared that the timber came from the unusual trees that formed the copse. Where had the seeds come from that had grown into the trees? The house did not know because it had had no awareness in its dormant state, no memory.

'I fell to earth and the soil was good,' was the only answer Caleb was going to get to that question. The house likened the seeds to eggs, and the trees to caterpillars, in its life-cycle. Then along came a man who transformed it into a butterfly.

'How did you manage to persuade him to do that – in your caterpillar stage?'

'I am able to produce certain illusions . . . which appear real to people. He saw the possibilities. He was a younger man than you, with a fertile imagination. There was a woman he often dreamed about – she came to him after he fell asleep in the trees. Together they built the house – me. Without the man, however, I should not have been able to form the woman . . . I need the blueprint of a human mind.'

'What about a companion for me?'

'You have not yet earned one.'

When Caleb asked where the original occupants had gone, the house became evasive. It was the first time it had shown any weakness of character. Caleb sensed a terrible secret behind this caginess and pressed the house for a reply. Finally the reply came and Caleb was horrified.

'You *worked* him to death,' he cried. There was a rustle from the eaves: not birds, but discomfort.

'He was . . . weaker than I thought. His strength failed him. I am most sincerely sorry.'

It was an ugly tale but Caleb had learned something: the house was able to feel compassion. Presumably the woman, being a product of the builder's imagination, disappeared with his death. The following morning Caleb tested this streak of compassion, to his own cost. He refused to work. Suddenly the beam above his head began spinning, the rope winding around it at a speed almost too fast to follow. In a few seconds Caleb was on tiptoe, his neck stretching slightly with his own weight.

'You will do as you are told,' said the house, 'or you will hang.'

After that incident there was an understanding between them, if not rapport.

Sometime later Caleb asked the house what had become of the corpse. He was told that the body had been taken down by the roots of the house. Caleb suppressed a shudder. So the house had roots, like a tree. It produced an ugly picture in his mind. The thing that held him prisoner was like a giant, static octopus, with grey tentacles that reached down into the earth, from which it obtained its food and moisture. It could grow its own parts but needed the man to fashion its limbs: shave them, smooth them with sandpaper and finally wax them to a polished finish. The house would brook no other visitors. No birds settled in its eaves, nor mice in its walls. It would not have furniture touching its glossed floors and glass was forbidden. Not a cockroach settled in a crack that was not instantly crushed.

Caleb reluctantly admitted to himself that he too received some

benefit from the situation. Waxing and polishing wood can be
very therapeutic. Mindless, yes, but soothing. Caleb found the
physical exercise eased his stress and he felt better than he had
done for years. His parents had died some months earlier in a gas
explosion in their London flat. They had left him a certain
amount of money: enough to purchase the caravan site he had
always wanted. He had been on his way down to the Cornish
coast to view prospective sites when he had become lost on the
moor. The rest of his relatives lived in Derbyshire and he rarely
contacted them anyway. There had been a girl once, a couple of
years previously, but that had fizzled out when he had shown no
interest in marriage. There was no one who would miss him – not
for a long while – and, when he came to think about it seriously,
he had no real desire to rush back into the mainstream of life. It
was just . . . just this idea that he was not a free man any longer. It
was a degrading experience and as soon as he could he was going
to get away.

He learned that the house was vulnerable. Once, when he was
out by the copse, sawing wood and stacking it so that it would
season, he reached up quickly to untie the rope from his neck.
The house was quicker. It dragged him, choking, a hundred feet
along the ground. Afterwards Caleb could smell burning where
the beam had spun and the friction had heated its ends. The
house was incensed and Caleb realised, not without feeling a
certain amount of perverse pleasure, that the house was afraid of
fire.

A house with roots was, at the same time, fascinating and
grotesque. Caleb had no difficulty in imagining the tentacles
gripping earth and flints below his feet. Ugly, hairy limbs,
corpse-grey in their world of tangible darkness. Dead things were
buried in such darknesses, not living creatures. It was like having
one's legs deep in the dirt and clay, held fast in a world of
sightless worms. Real trees were different. They did not have the
power of thought. Their extremities were at home amongst
inanimate rocks. But the house was . . . yes, like *him*. It was a
feeling, thinking creature and it was difficult to consider it
otherwise.

One evening, as a large, orange sun was slipping gradually
down behind the horizon, Caleb was sitting on the porch steps

enjoying a few minutes rest. He asked the house the name of the former occupant.

'His name? Jacober. Joachim Jacober. I remember he was something to do with farming. A good carpenter though.'

Caleb smiled wryly. 'The house that Jack built.'

The house asked him to explain the remark and Caleb told him the tale. The house was intrigued and asked for more stories and Caleb obliged it with other tales involving houses: The Three Little Pigs, Hansel and Gretel and The Little Old Woman That Lived in A Shoe. After the story-telling was over Caleb got to thinking how much humans had come to regard their homes as personalities in their own right. They cared for them like pets, lavishing money and time on beautifying them. In some cases they almost worshipped them. There had been a time when the owner of a stately home would die rather than relinquish his property. Was his, Caleb's, situation any different from theirs? Only in the fact that he had no choice.

A few dry leaves blew across the porch and rested for an instant or two against Caleb's boots. The first signs of autumn were evident in the air. Birds were becoming restless and the ground animals were beginning to look around them nervously, as if searching for secure defences against the coming winter. Caleb knew there was a place for a fire in one of the back rooms of the house: it was that creature's one concession to human needs, thought Caleb. Well, perhaps not the only one, but there were precious few comforts to be had around the house. He wondered if the house would permit a rocking chair, providing it was made of the same wood as the rest of it? Probably not. Was it even worth asking?

The evening sky was covered in purple blemishes now, like dark bruises on a pale face. A boxer's face. Caleb was not a fighter. He did not have the aggressive make-up of that type of man. But he was stubborn, like a rock or a tree stump, and he had reached the end of his tolerance.

'I'm not working for you any more,' he said in a firm voice, 'unless I get certain concessions. You need me now. I want a rocking chair, freedom from this rope . . . and company.'

For a few moments there was only the sound of the wind whispering to the corner of the house. Then came an unexpected reply. 'You will also need provisions for the winter – blankets, warm clothing, fuel and food. It is time you went into the nearest town.'

Caleb, who had been expecting a threat of some kind, was taken aback by this reply. He reached up gingerly and began to untie the knot in the rope. There was no sign of movement from the house, no retaliation.

'How will I get into town?' he asked. 'The battery to my car is flat and I'm out of petrol.'

'You will find fuel for the motor car in a pit covered by a board and earth, at the back of the copse. Have you any ideas regarding the battery? I'm not familiar with the function of this item.'

Caleb explained that they could try using the rope and beam method to pull the car along in gear and get it started that way. The house agreed.

'Aren't you worried I won't come back to you?' asked Caleb.

'You will not live through the winter without the necessary stocks. I do not wish to be the cause of another death. I must take the chance that you have grown to regard me with some ... affection. Besides, I am not finished with you yet. There is something else I wish to show you before you leave.'

'You would have hung me,' accused Caleb, a little bitterly.

'No. With you the threat was enough. I would never have carried it to its conclusion.'

Conjecture on what was, or what was not the truth behind the words, was pointless. Caleb accepted the words, although some doubt remained in his mind and would always do so. He went out to the rear of the house and found the petrol. Presumably this had been originally stored by Jacober for use in the truck that now stood rusting near the copse. He took one of the jerry cans and filled the tank of his car. Then he removed the wooden spear from its flank, leaving a hole the size of a football. Finally, he tied the end of the rope to the bumper, ready for the following morning when the house would attempt to start the car.

The gloom had descended but there was enough light to discern the vague outline of the spinney and as Caleb walked towards the veranda he was instructed by the house to pay close attention to the trees. One of them, a small sapling, trembled, its leaves rustling like tin foil in the still evening. There was a stream that ran around the back of the house and curved in towards the copse. Tongues of water leaped from the brook and splashed around the roots of the youthful tree. Spray filled the air as fine as mist and through this veil stepped the tree, white-limbed, dark-haired and with eyes the deep purple of damsons. She was beautiful.

The young woman walked slowly towards him. He recognised her of course, not as someone he had once known, but as the woman he had always dreamed of meeting and falling in love with. She climbed the steps, barefooted, and Caleb stood, over-awed by the dark eyes, the high cheekbones, the skin as delicate as magnolia blossom. Her slim hands reached up and rested on his shoulders.

'Now we can *really* talk to each other,' she said, 'and afterwards we shall lie together . . . you and I.'

Caleb's throat felt dry. The house, the copse, the woman by his side – they were all one and the same. He knew now why the house was so confident that he would return. They needed each other. They filled a hollow in each other's lives.

The two lovers lay in each others arms and watched the moon climb the wall of the night sky. Caleb could feel her heartbeat against his own: measured the minutes by its pace. He knew exactly what to say to her because he understood her so well: not only was she part of the house, she was also part of Caleb – the perfect link between them. She was the catalyst to bring about the fusion of two spirits foreign to one another. They talked well into the small hours of the next day, about their plans for the future and the events of the past, their hands constantly touching each other, testing the reality of illusion.

The following morning the woman had gone but her spiritual presence remained. Her soft limbs had solidified to wood and her skin to silver bark, but she was there, at the entrance to the copse, beckoning with her leaves. She would be waiting for him when he returned.

Once the car was ready Caleb instructed the house to tow it while he sat inside slipping the clutch. After two or three attempts the motor started and Caleb left it running on full choke while he re-entered the house. He stood just inside the doorway and ran his hand over the polished wooden banister. His eyes took in the solid hallway, the panelled walls with the grain flowing gloriously in brown rivers to the archways of the roof. Knots and whorls turned the currents into spiral eddies. The house *was* beautiful in its own form. Its timbers were fashioned to perfection. Its doors and frames were perfectly flush with one another – wooden hinges held by wooden pegs, well oiled and smooth-working. Perfection, yet ... without exactitude. There was a rustic splendour to the rough-hewn beams that shouldered the roof – a balance but not precise symmetry.

He turned quickly, and left. 'I'll be back,' he said.

Caleb drove along the moor road carefully noting landmarks for his return journey. Finally he came to a signpost which directed him to the town. As he drove along he studied the scenery around him: mauve heather rippled like the gentle waves of wind-blown water as far as he could see. There were islands of gorse and broom too, and the occasional outcrop of rock like the blunt, grey snouts of porpoise breaking the surface.

He was only vaguely aware of the other vehicle. It turned the corner, hidden by a drystone wall, on the wrong side of the road. There was a moment when Caleb was conscious of the sound of metal on metal and a shower of brilliant sparks but this was rapidly followed by the blackness which washed over his incredible pain.

The other man was dead. He knew it, instinctively, upon waking. The terror he had seen in that face could only be a prelude to death. His own pain was his reminder that he was alive. Other events, the coming and going of medical staff, were blurred and disjointed, both in time and action. They moved around him in a haze of grey light, like attendant ghosts. He tried to remain attentive to his own life-force, his own *being*. After all, he thought, pain is only the centralisation, the concentration of *feeling*. While he could still feel he would still be alive. *I feel, therefore I am,* he thought. By the time he was able to think clearly he realised he had been in the hospital for many months. Four, they told him. His requests to be discharged were, he knew, premature. They stemmed from a desire and though he voiced them frequently over the next few weeks, he knew he was not well enough to face a journey across the moor.

During the days that followed, he drifted in and out of dreams and wakefulness. One of his relatives, an uncle, came down from Derby to visit him. Apparently his aunt had already been down once but Caleb had not been conscious at the time. He thanked his uncle but said further visits would be unnecessary: the journey was expensive and there was not a great deal of money in the family. Caleb assured his uncle he was very much on the mend in any case.

There came a time when he began to hear the sounds of summer outside his window. He got up that day and went for a short walk in the hospital grounds. It was not the first time he had been out of bed but they had not allowed him outside before then. In the gardens the wildlife was busy with its mid-year tasks. Caleb suddenly became determined to leave within a short time. Closeted in his ward he had managed to fight the urge to return to the house but once in the fresh air, witness to all the activity of the outdoors, he began to feel guilty about spending his life in idleness. The house was probably missing him and no doubt needed his hands to repair whatever damage the ravages of winter had inflicted upon it. From that day forth his physiotherapy programme was accelerated and he set himself definite goals.

Finally the day came when the hospital authorities agreed to let him go. He ordered a chauffeur-driven car to take him back to the house. On the way he stopped off for provisions ... and a rocking chair which the driver reluctantly allowed to occupy the back seat. As they travelled over the moor Caleb chattered to the driver. When they were about halfway there the driver suddenly became a little nervous.

'You talk about this house of yours as if it was some kind of a ... friend,' said the man, keeping his eyes fixed to the road.

'Well, it is in a way. Don't you regard your car as a companion of sorts? You call it *she*.'

'That's just a figure of speech, init? I mean, it's just a hunk of metal and tubes really.'

'But you're fond of it.'

'I s'pose so,' replied the man. A little later on he said, 'Just out of hospital, ain't you?'

'You know I am. You picked me up.'

'Could've been one of the doctors,' the driver murmured. After that both men remained quiet.

As they drew near to the large dwelling, with its old-fashioned porch and wooden railings, Caleb sensed that something was not quite right. Something had been lost. Lustre? Yes, that was it. The house was like a seashell that had lost its creature. It still shone, but there was a lack of life about it. He climbed out of the car.

'I'm back,' he called. There was no response. 'House, I've come back.'

The driver got out and carefully unloaded the things from the boot and back seat, keeping one eye on Caleb all the time. When he had finished he climbed back into the car.

'My money,' he said.

Caleb absently took out his wallet and stuffed some notes into the man's hand, then entered the house. He called again, but his words echoed in the hallway: a hollow, empty sound.

He touched a doorpost. It felt dry and without substance. The house had always had a *heavy* look and feel about it: solid, oakish. Now it was a husk without strength. A fibrous thing. No juices were running through its frame, filling its muscular wooden shoulders with supple strength. He went round to the back but the stream was still running strongly. It had not been lack of water. He took a spade and began digging, near to the house. After a few moments he came to a root: a withered, brittle limb attached to the corner of the building.

Returning to where the driver sat in the car, he said, 'Dead. I think it died of despair. It thought I wasn't coming back again.'

'I see,' said the driver, carefully. The man started the motor of the car. Just then there was a rustle from the copse, as if a wind had just sprung up amongst the leaves of the trees. An idea occurred to Caleb. He picked up the axe he had just bought, from amongst the goods the driver had unloaded.

'Perhaps if we grafted an extension,' Caleb said. 'You know, added a room at the back? Maybe then the rest of the house would take on life again. It might work.'

The driver's eyes never left the axe as he gradually eased the car forward, round, and back onto the road again. He took one last look at Caleb and then the house, before driving off quickly in the direction he had come.

Caleb set to work immediately on the extension, handling the freshly cut trees lovingly, once they were down. He wanted to hear those resonant tones again before the summer was out. He missed the timbre of that rich voice. There was also someone else he missed very much and without the house she would never return.

He studied the weather-boarding of the exterior of the house, in order that the extension should match the rest of the building. The boards were fixed horizontally to the uprights of the house and chamfered at an angle of 45 degrees at the lower edge. This, he knew, was for protection against rain and gales but at the top edge they were tapered solely for elegance. The wood had also been resinated.

The roof would be difficult. On the sloping ends there were stepped gables of wood which provided protection against the weather at the point where the walls and roof met but overlaying the lapped wooden tiles of the roof was a thatch of heather held in place by ropes and weighted with stones. It was this particular feature which would give him the most trouble. He saw now that his initial image of the house as a New England farm was only an overall impression: in fact the house was a hotch-potch of styles, unique in its architecture but managing somehow to retain the flavour of rustic good taste. Anyway, he liked it. Once again he gave Joachim Jacober a mental salute for managing to blend the several characteristics of separate design features into something aesthetically pleasing yet functional and hardy.

For a man with no training – no formal training – as a carpenter or builder the prospect of adding the extension might be a daunting one. Yet inside Caleb was a strong sense of longing mixed with an enthusiasm for the work. These two powerful agents would see him over any practical problems he might encounter. He had his eyes and could inspect the main building whenever he came across a stumbling block. He would do it if it killed him. He *had* to do it. He had already invested a large part of his soul in the house.

For two weeks he worked solidly, pausing only for sleep and food. At the end of that time he was exhausted but had enough planks to begin the extension. He did wonder, once or twice, whether the chauffeur would say anything to the people at the hospital about him, but no one came so Caleb guessed the man must have confined his tale to the public bar of his local.

Towards the end of summer, the new room was complete. Caleb admired it from every angle and carefully put his tools away in the hope that he would need them again. Then he took his rocking chair and placed it gently on the porch. It was an evening as fine and soft as pink blossom. The moor was streaked with dark avenues of magenta where the dying sun levelled its last rays. There was optimism in the air: Caleb could sense it stirring amongst the heather and grasses of the dips and hollows of the moorland. The bracken was alive with hope. He settled back in the chair, rocking gently, his eyes upon a single, slender tree in the spinney not far from where he sat. Perhaps it would not be too long ...

Jessica Amanda Salmonson lives in
Seattle, Washington, and won the World
Fantasy Award for her anthology
Amazons. A specialist in Japanese folklore
she has also written several popular novels
featuring strong female warrior characters
including *The Swordswoman*.

Hode of the High Place

Jessica Amanda Salmonson

A single monument marked the expanse of dry prairie: one inexplicable mountainous block on a flat terrain. At its top sprouted what looked to be a castle of twisted spires and leaning towers. People of the farm community of Ausper, which lay in the morning shadows of the monolith, claimed that no one but the eagles nesting in the hollow of the towers lived in those heights, nor had anyone lived there in the past. Yet for all the seeming randomness of the peculiar cluster, even a fool would have to see there had been purpose behind the composition. Therefore, the few strangers who ventured to Ausper generally found themselves prompted to query as to what unhuman workers built the bold structure at such an elevation. When so queried, the farmers would mutter a hoarse reply, mingled with a cough, muffled in cropped beards, and aimed into soiled hands, so that their answers were garbled and unclear. If asked kindly to repeat it, the response would again be murmured unintelligibly. If asked a third time what they said, the people displayed a tendency to provocation and would snap aloud, 'Thou are a deaf fool! Clean thine ears or ask no more questions!'

The truth of the matter, as one might guess, was that they had no real answers. Those lofty spires with round blank windows had been there since before the founding of Ausper. The oldest local legends offered no theory as to how the High Place came to be.

Peasant-minded farmers curtailed any predisposition to curiosity, keeping their attention on the begrudging soil and never on the eerie backdrop. Yet one fragile youth named Hode had noticed the High Place before he learned to walk, and never ceased to be fascinated by the steep cliffs and the eagles gliding around slender spires. When tiny, he had been so often scolded for asking about the inauspicious monument that he quickly

learned never to speak of the private determinations which were
unfashionable among his superstitious people.

Ausper lay far from any major metropoli, yet occasionally folk
ventured from beyond the prairie with no better goal in mind than
an enigmatic mountain with a crown of spires. Hode recalled a
time when three such wayfarers came riding in on lumbering
oxen. They were not mere sightseers come to gawk. They
intended to assault the elevated fortification.

One was a poet who sought to do a thing courageous so that his
verse would live after him, recounting the torture and turmoil of
his own heroic life. Upon arrival in Ausper, he gazed up into the
cloudless sky and saw how pointed steeples seemed to pierce the
noon sun, and the poet cried, 'We would be burnt by heaven's
golden orb if to that loft we ascend!' He fled in search of more
plausible ventures about which to compose vainglorious poetry.

The second was a poor and paunchy merchant who fancied
himself a wise and wily businessman. His aspiration was to climb
up and throw down what treasures must have been left in so safe a
keep. But when face to face with the looming escarpment, he went
purple around the jowls and wept that he would not survive to
invest the waiting fortune. With a spur of his ox he was off to
rejoin the poet and seek less deadly gain.

The remaining was a warrior named Sarx-unlo the Wizard
Killer, who laughed at the parting cravens, for he alone was the
true adventurer. He sat on the edge of the village nearest the
monument and surveyed his foe while gnawing on a bit of dried ox
meat. His dumb animal forged the coarse weeds between the
saguaro cacti which separated Ausper from the massive rock.
Here was also where Hode came upon occasion to scan the heights
with discerning eye, and now he ventured out from where he had
hidden when the three strangers approached. He joined the
warrior in wishful endeavour.

When Hode asked why a man with fighter's stance would come
to this insignificant land, Sarx-unlo answered that 'stone is a more
sturdy adversary than any man' or words to that effect. When
asked what gain there was in ascending treacherous cliffs, the
adventurer prattled about imagined rewards, including the good
chance of slaying the sorcerous hermit he imagined should reside
in such a citadel. Hode only half listened to the man who boasted

of being the famed Wizard Killer, of whom Hode had never heard. His thoughts were elsewhere than with the bragging warrior. Momentarily he interrupted: 'One day I shall be master of the High Place!' That announcement caused swarthy Sarx-unlo to laugh and slap his knee. But as he offered Hode a piece of ox meat, the Wizard Killer spoke in seriousness: 'If it be pre-ordained, then master of the High Place ye shall be.'

Subsequently Sarx-unlo died at the base of the cliff, and Hode could not say he was disappointed. He would have been jealous had another man reached the High Place. Yet the warrior's attempt struck iron to the flint heart of a common farm boy, and Hode was pressed to a firm resolve that someday he would succeed where stronger men had failed.

He scaled piles of fallen rock to see where the warrior, after his unscreaming plunge, had landed in an unusually contorted heap. Near the place where Sarx-unlo fell, Hode spied a small entry to a cavern. He fetched the undamaged sword from the mangled mess which had been Sarx-unlo, and used it as lever to move rocks away from the nearly buried hole. Then he crawled in a short distance but was repelled by the odour of bat droppings and the glum quietude. After memorising the location of the uneasily attained entrance and leaving the sword propped there as marker, Hode fled homeward.

Many days passed. His every waking notion, his very dreams and nightmares, even his mastubatory fantasies were obsessed with an undiminishing desire to ascend to those black, bleak towers. Yet he was also frightened, for he knew himself a mere child, smaller and less strong than others his age. Surely the High Place would laugh at him more easily than it had done to Sarx-unlo the Wizard Killer.

One midday as Hode's mother set steaming broth before husband and son, she remarked that the boy had eaten birdlike and was growing more introverted in direct proportion to his becoming more gaunt. Her husband motioned her to silence and said every growing child passes through a lethargic period and Hode would outgrow his. He patted the boy on the shoulder. But secretly he fretted as did his wife, for Hode had always been sickly and weaklings did not live long lives in rough country.

Later Hode and his father were working the dusty fields, but

Hode was not much help. His attention was averted from tasks at hand, drawn to the unnatural architecture of the High Place. Never before had his father scolded him for uselessness, but this day the burden of the boy was heavier than usual. He had rationed Hode the lightest of chores, yet even these went unfinished. This on top of the unproductive soil, a rainless summer, and unfattened barn fowl caused Hode's father to break down under the pressures. Always pampered because of his inadequacy, Hode did not take well to the belittling spiel his father set upon him.

That night, the father went to apologise for calling his son all manner of unmanly names, but Hode was not to be found. He had filled a wooden bucket with food, fire-flint, other survival necessities, and run away. His mother wailed that her only child would be eaten by prairie beasts. The guilt-ridden father vowed that he would go in search of Hode, never to give up until either the boy's bones were found or he was safely re-instated with his family.

In the centre of the vast, fetid cavern, Hode built a fire. He sat on a blunt stalagmite watching a thin strand of smoke waft upward into the darkness of the ceiling. Here, he thought with deranged casualness, he would live forever, feasting on plump bats plucked from their roosts like pears on a cactus bush, drinking the limestone water that drip-dropped from the points of blue-hued stalactites, hunting for sparse twigs and cactus roots for his fires only on the darkest nights, never again to venture into the light of day.

He sat plotting amid the azure forest of stupendous teeth like a parasite in the maw of a colossal sphinx. He watched the dancing shadows of the firelight jump and reel like a thousand demons behind weird rock formations. That night and the following day he sat thus, until he adjusted to the chamber and gained a sense of belonging which he had never experienced in his parents' sod house.

When it grew dark outside on the second day, he ventured into the night to collect a store of burnable fuel. Before the early hours had brought the sun, he'd also fashioned a bed in a wall depression, using the brown, lichenous moss which survived in the crags at the base of the cliffs. He slept through the daylight hours and awoke on that night, adapting with uncanny swiftness to nocturnal habits.

On that third night he heard his father's call for the first of many occasions. It was unlikely that the wandering torch-bearer would find the cave entrance and less likely that he'd enter so dark a place if he did stumble upon it. Yet Hode waited fearful of discovery, until his father's mournful calling waned with distance and was gone. Soon, Hode reasoned, he would be pronounced devoured by some flatland predator and be forgotten after minimal lamentation. In the meanwhile, he'd have to be careful not to be spotted on his night sorties for firewood. Later, when the villagers were convinced he was lost forever, he might risk stealing some of his needs from them. For now, he must leave no clues to his status.

For Hode, the monument had always been a fetish of sorts, and he experienced great sexual stimulus from being within the cavern. On the fourth day, as he lay in his bed of coarse moss, Hode attained puberty, for, upon his usual orgasm, semen and sperm spurted into his hand. Hode looked at the substance with curiosity and childish fear, wondering if it were normal that a cheesy unguent should exude from himself. He wiped it on his filthy jerkin, then lay back expressionless.

Unknown to Hode, the scent of his fertility had trailed into the deeper caverns where it aroused the sensitive olfactories of an underworld inhabitant. Something was setting the bats of the downward passage a-flurry. In a few moments the sound of the upset was nearer. Panicked winged rodents fluttered up from the pits, through Hode's private lair, out into the day.

Hode sat up, knowing it was unnatural for bats to flee into the light. They should remain roosted, sleeping even as Hode was prepared to do. The event of their rackety passing was cause for concern. Hode was about to flee after them when he caught the sound of a siren-song which was at once repulsive in tenor yet attractive for its unduplicable melody. As one captivated in a dream, Hode dropped from the wall depression and wove between the blue stalagmites. The only passage from the chamber besides the outside exit was one which led downward at a sharp angle. Hode had never acquired the fortitude to explore the lower regions, for his aspirations led up and not down. But now he found himself walking into those depths, mesmerised by sardonic, demonic music.

A cold gust rushed up from the lower levels, rank with a

metallic pungency. Freezing though the wind was, Hode smiled foolishly and felt warm in the womb of the monument. The passage grew steeper and narrower. Ember-light was left behind. Then, with a suddenness that made Hode jerk to a stop, the beckoning piping ceased and, as Hode shook his head, confused and woozy, he realised the length of his toes hung over a ledge that, for all his vision could tell, might be a bottomless pit. Shaken by the nearness of his demise, and free of the enticing metre, he turned and fled, stumbling, scrabbling, back to his chamber, and wedged himself deep in the depression where his bed was made. He curled into a ball and irrationally felt safe from harm.

During his waking hours there was little to do. But after several days Hode discovered a method by which to amuse himself. He found that in striking a stalactite with the broad edge of Sarx-unlo's sword, the stalactite could be set to musical reverberation. With experimentation, he found that each stone spear had a bell-toll distinctly its own. In gleeful exultation, Hode ran wildly through the chamber, striking every stalatite that hung in reach and leaping to reach higher ones. A tuneless melody was brought to a near-deafening roar. Bats fled the chamber as Hode leapt and parried about, swinging sword against rock time after time, giving no toll a chance to die away. The whole of the mountainous monument was reverberating and the people of Ausper awoke that night to an awesome drone.

Enthralled by his mischievous caper, Hode did not notice that the bases of several large stalactites were beginning to crack, their roots weakened by vibration. With unsuspected good fortune, he tired of his game before bringing stone tusks upon himself.

When the ruckus died away, one sound remained, and Hode's gaiety was ungulfed by dread. The nightmarish siren-song had come again, as on the first night of his fertility. This time he heard the echoes not from unknown depths but near at hand.

Weary from the recent exertion, it was even more difficult to maintain the will needed to disobey the caller in the passage. With hands clapped to ears, Hode hummed loudly so as not to hear the beckoning. Not to be foiled, the creature emerged from the passage. Hode could not make it out from his vantage point. Anxious and fearful, he kicked a chunk of dried cactus on the fire lest he be cast in darkness, then climbed into the imagined protection of his bed in the wall.

The song had died to a snuffling. Hode lowered his hands from his ears and tried to guess by sound where the elusive intruder was. It flowed from one hiding place to another and Hode could not tell the place of a sound's origin from its echo. He caught rare glimpses of a shapeless form melding from shadow to shadow. He waited and watched and listened in his depression, afraid, seeing nothing certain, pressed flat upon his hard bed, wishing he were invisible. Then, suddenly, the water bucket he'd set beneath a stalactite to capture water for drinking fell, or was thrown, with a splash and a sizzle, dousing the fire. The cavern was cast instantly into indigo darkness. Hode slunk back into the recesses of his bed-hole.

The sound was dreadfully close: immediately below the rim of his bed. Hode whimpered, then forced himself to be silent, wondering why he had dropped Sarx-unlo's sword when he covered his ears. Weaponless and witless, he realised the demon had climbed onto the shelf he had foolishly believed inviolate. He heard it sniffling about like a drippy-nosed hog; nearer, nearer, until a wet, cold appendage touched his leg. It clamped hold of him!

He screamed, squeaked, kicked, fought, begged, but these actions died into whimpering panic. A gelatinous mass flowed over him, oblivious to his thrashing, smothering him as the water had smothered the flames. Then he felt something expected and pleasant: gentle, rhythmic constrictions around his genitals. The sweet, weird siren song came again, higher-pitched and more excited, penetrating his mind, lulling him emotionally, draining him physically, leaving him at last to writhe alone, longing for the return of ecstasy but somehow knowing the demon had taken what it wanted and would never come again.

For two days he lay unmoving, as one who has lost his beloved and is robbed of passion. He did not rise to build a fire or to drink, nor did he strangle bats to feast upon. His spare frame grew more skeletal. With his hair so wild, his clothes so ragged, he looked like a hideous devil-doll of a voodoo worker lain in the depression of a cavern wall. Eventually he began to raise his spirit from the depths of apathy where it had been abandoned by the demanding ectoplasmic organism. On wobbling legs he climbed off his bed to build a fire. He put all his wood on it and burnt even the bucket which lay atop the previous burnings, so that he would have a larger than usual blaze to chase away his fears and thaw his succubus-chilled emotions.

As the fire grew bright, Hode bent his head back beneath a stalactite to catch a few drops of bitter liquid. His head thus upturned, waiting patiently for one slow-to-come drop after the next, he mindlessly watched smoke trail up between upside-down rock formations. With the blaze built so large, the chamber's highest reaches were rendered dimly visibly. Hode saw a narrow, black fissure through which the smoke escaped, and a procession of logic went slowly through his muddled mind, his own voice saying: 'If this mountain is unscalable from outside, the route to the High Place must be through the innards of this big rock!'

Truly, truly, he reasoned, struck with absurd happiness: he need only climb into that fissure to go where the smoke goes!

In that idea was an obvious problem, for he was not smoke. What sort of creature could scale the slick walls, or clamber up the conical stalactites, or walk upside down upon the ceiling? It would be no task to fall into the pits toward deeper caverns; but how would a body go about falling up into the higher levels?

While he was working these thoughts through, a disturbance at the cavern entryway went unnoticed. The first he realised he was no longer alone was when he heard his name cried: 'Hode!' He looked between stone growths to where his father stood with flickering torch casting shadows to oppose those of the campfire.

'By all the gods I knew thou hadst to live!' he exclaimed, advancing with an open arm.

Hode stumbled backward, eyes wide with what might have been fright or despair. His secret cave was discovered! It was a woeful moment indeed, to be hauled back to where he would no longer be master of himself, where everyone thought him feeble, no longer to be surrounded by these fabulous stone walls. He fell over the blunt stalagmite and lay on his back screaming over and over this piercing command: 'Leave me alone! Leave me alone! Leave me alone!'

The concerned father came closer, fearing his infirm offspring now suffered a malady worse than others: madness. Above the interloper's head a stalactite, which had been weakened at its roots days before when Hode batted it repeatedly into music, began to loosen under the echoes of the boy's shrill, repetitious cry.

The father had only time to hear a cracking sound and look up. He dropped his torch, tried vainly to deflect the falling spear with both hands, but was pressed to the floor and pierced through the chest. The tall, slender stalactite began to tip like a falling saguaro, and struck other stalactites with booming force. These were broken loose in turn and fell against others, which broke and fell against still others. Around Hode, huge missiles were falling and chipping against stalagmites on the floor. It was the second night the folk of Ausper awoke to the sound of the mother-of-bells, and they were sore afraid, for this time it was louder. The calamitous bumping was far noisier than Hode had been able to conjure with one small sword, and the resultant roar burst his eardrums. He viewed the catastrophe in utter silence. Huge, unsounding teeth fell around him.

It lasted scant moments and, miraculously, Hode was un-crushed, his only wounds betrayed by the blood trickling from each ear. He crawled about the rubble of broken, split, chipped and otherwise damaged stalactites and stalagmites. The exit from the cavern had been sealed by one fallen formation, but Hode did not care. He made his way over and under things to where his father lay squashed and impaled, and was a little disappointed to find him dead and not suffering. Frustration was soon erased, however, for he looked up along that first stalactite to fall and saw that its top leaned upon a partially crushed crop of small, close-packed stalactites. To the left of these he could see the edge of the dark fissure.

Inspired by his fortune, Hode ascended the angle of the long, tall stone, like a willowy shadow in the flickering light of the diminishing fire. From the ragged top of the inverted cone, he reached one of the sapling stalactites and pulled himself toward the ceiling, clinging like an ape. He reached to another down-probing spear, then another, and made his way to the narrow crack which led up. There was a lip on the fissure and he climbed onto it, breathing hard from the strain. He sat there a long while, swinging his legs back and forth from the heights. When his breath was captured, he braced himself on each side of the chasm and began to wriggle upward. It was a difficult task, but what he lacked in muscle he bolstered with a perverse will. For half an hour he strained and grunted, making what seemed to be slow progress, coughing the musty air of the ages, having no sense of hearing and no light to guide him, depending solely on the sense of touch to get him safely on.

When he came to a higher level, he crawled onto the new floor, panting heavily, unable to rise for a long time.

Here there grew a wondrous, unearthly garden of glowing fungi, more like stupendous moulds than mushrooms, red and gold in coloration, with spore-heads of even more dazzling brilliance. Though it was foreboding in appearance, Hode reasoned that this garden had provided domestic fruit to whatever human or semi-human beings once lived in the castle that still waited above. Famished, he broke off the golden, glowing head of a twisted fungus and bit into it as if it were a melon of known origin. It tasted reasonably good. He tried several others. The dry ones which had gone to spore no longer glowed, and tasted like wood; but the moist ones were delicacies which quenched thirst as well as hunger. The dry spore-heads, he imagined, would make good fuel should he choose to build a fire.

Delicate phosphorescent insects lived amid the night-plants: hard-shelled pollinators brighter than gems; minuscule predators of hideous, mandibled countenance; fiery bright inchworms making whimsical progress up the sides of stems; and large, exquisitely fragile butterflies with feathery antennae and bright amber eyes. Here also foraged hexapod tortoises with white lantern spots decorating their carapaces. Hode surmised that these six-legged reptiles, like the fungi, were once the foodstuff of the vanished society. There were none of the bats of the lower levels, as this was a new ecology that had formerly been cultivated but now grew independent of caretakers.

Strengthened by the pastry-light fungi, Hode quested beyond the colourful garden and quickly found a tunnel which spiralled upward. His heart leapt when he found it, for this would certainly take him to the High Place.

Yet he did not immediately enter. A fear sprung up within him which could not be blamed on the eeriness of his surroundings.

Here he stood on the threshold of his goal, and he feared that, once it was attained, there would be no more purpose to his selfish, miserable life. What would he find above but vast, empty corridors and helix stairwells to tower rooms? For the first time he recognised that the possession of an object was never as ecstatic as the seeking; the reality never as pleasurable as the dream.

These were fearful revelations, more frightening than when he was demon-raped, worse than the rain of stalactites. This was an intangible fear that could not be faced physically. It was difficult to overcome a thing that could not be seen or touched, yet he did overcome these feelings and threw himself forward into the tunnel. Round and round and up and up the passage led until he came to the final bend, greeted by a form of light which had become alien to his retina: sunlight. He shaded his eyes with an arm, saw a huge brown eagle take flight from a sloppily constructed nest and vanish through a round window.

Blinking and squinting watery eyes, Hode peered down from the High Place, seeing the whole village of sod houses – a handful of lumps cast like dice on a dry plain – interwoven with ploughed acreage and miserable weedy crops that seemed little greener than the harsh land which stretched to the horizon. Saguaros stood below like stick-man sentinels.

Here in the High Place Hode decided to stay, for there was nowhere else to go and no place he'd rather be. He turned from the round port and inspected the eagles' nest built on an obsidian daïs. Within he saw three featherless eaglets with curved, open beaks, squawking and begging for food, looking back at him from ugly purple eyes in oversized heads. They flopped about within the confines of their poorly made nest, exercising tiny undeveloped wings. Hode could not hear their baby-bird noises, but was sure of the raspiness because he felt their cries vibrating in his chest.

These three might become magnificent hunters and flyers someday, but now they were awkward and ugly. Hode felt an affinity toward them. He pointed his fingers at them and they made harmless efforts to eat each digit. For the first time in his life, Hode laughed for the joy of a living thing. They would swallow a finger to the last knuckle, regurgitate it as untasty, carefully eye the selection, then try another.

In his deafness, with blood still encrusting his punctured ears, Hode did not hear the flap of large wings at his back. He only felt a quick breeze from the window and paid it no heed until the talons of the mother bird were in his neck.

The bird complained harshly as Hode clamoured about the room, groaning and beating furiously at the squawking bird attached to his back. Despite the noise, to Hode it was a nightmare in silence. He did not even hear his own scream when the great bird brought her curved beak down from over his shoulder and mutilated his right eye. She pulled it out by the roots, swallowing it after it dangled in her beak a moment.

The beak came down for the other eye. But Hode caught the neck in both hands and proceeded to twist and strangle. Her claws remained firm in his shoulders, her wings beating violently, until she managed to lift scrawny Hode off the floor. Both fighters fell as one when the bird grew weak with no oxygen passing through clenched lungs. She flopped a little more, but Hode kept the stranglehold for several hours after the last throes of death were over, until he passed into coma, later to awaken with the promise of an eagle breakfast.

Some of the slain bird he fed raw to the youngsters. The rest he cooked over the dried, woody fungi in a dome-shaped oven he discovered in an area of the castle that once had been a kitchen.

Numb to pain, he was not agitated by his mangled eye socket as he explored the myriad spires. All but one was devoid of anything of interest. In the highest of the high spires, he found a tiny chamber containing a thing he feared even to gaze upon, much less touch. He scurried down the countless stairs, blocking what he had seen from his mind, and did not venture that way again for many years.

Slowly he readjusted to diurnal habits. He'd descend periodically into the fungoid gardens for food, both turtle and vegetable, and would also capture insects to feed his three wards, who soon gained pinfeathers. The insects, along with scraps and guts of tortoises, kept the beggars strong and swift to grow.

In the months to follow, Hode's socket healed so completely that one might have thought him born with but one organ of sight. His pets grew large and sturdy. He trained them to attack other birds nesting in the cliffs below the castle, including other eagles. They even took to fetching lizards from the prairie, and an occasional rodent or rabbit. The whole family ate well and of a variety of dishes. The three wards became magnificent specimens, sinister on account of their training, while Hode alone remained small and ugly.

It happened by accident that one eagle fetched up a newborn girl, kicking and crying, pierced and bloody. Hode, delighted by this unholy feast, praised the eagle and said no meat had ever been more tasty. The other two eagles were jealous of the attention lavished on the first. On each of the following two days, they in turn flew up to the castle with babies snatched fresh from their cradles. Hode gave no thought to the panic roused in the village. Indeed, his only thought on the subject of Ausper was that in a town so small, three babies were probably all there were, and he'd not have another on his supper table for a while.

But the birds were undaunted in their desire to please their master. Two of them together managed to mutilate and kill a young man of strapping dimensions and carry his carcase to the castle. Hode laughed and patted the two proud birds affectionately. Though he was tired of human flesh so regularly, he yet gained pleasure from the birds' efforts to maintain his approval. He did not cook this last body, but let the three birds have as much of it as they wanted, and the rest he threw out the window where it made the far descent to the growing scrap pile at the base of the cliff.

A party of men enraged by the eagle attacks happened upon the place where the bones of Hode's and the eagles' feasts clattered and splintered. These men were not wise, but it took no wisdom to deduce that most of the bones had been cooked. The men turned their eyes to those ghastly twisted spires with new dread. Their superstitious fears about the High Place were coming to fruition; and there wasn't even a way by which a brave man could reach the High Place to battle whatever nefarious creature had set up housekeeping there.

Hode, safe from the people, gave them no thought. Once, when a foolhardy villager attempted the impossible ascent, Hode did not wait for him to fall of his own accord, but in good spirits sent his eagles to yank the fellow from his grip and send him dashing to the rocky ground. Free as he was from law and retribution, Hode had no qualms about his ghastly acts, and no fear of reprisals.

Then came a day when his largest and preferred eagled flopped lamely through the window, a barn fowl in its grip, an arrow through its breast. For the first time Hode felt some of the misery suffered by the villagers. He nursed the bird, crying the whole time, giving it false praise for finding so fine a piece of poultry. It died with its head in his hands. As he walked lonely through the castle halls, the other two eagles banqueted on their brother, being birds and, after all, incapable of mourning.

A winding stairway led Hode to the tiny chamber where even he, small of height, could not stand erect. This was the one place in his domain where he never came, for there were dread runes over the archway leading in, and Hode, with no ability to read, feared the power of the written word. He feared this room as less monstrous men fear demons and darkness, but his fears were overcome by a mission of vengeance.

In the highest tower of the High Place, in a closet-sized room, upon an ebon table, there was a strange object carved from a single block of blood-crimson ruby. It was fashioned in the shape of a bone with a serpent wrapped around, the universal insignia used on jars of poison, pictured on no-trespassing signs to prove the warning adamant, and marked on maps to show where wayfarers had best not go. Previously Hode had been loath to touch the carving. Though forgotten to antiquity, he suspected this antique sceptre was the original source of the bone-serpent as a signal of corruption.

Hode's shaking hand gripped the foreboding sceptre and held it near his breast, waiting to see if he were stricken dead for contact with a base object. Discovering himself still alive, he gazed with his single eye into the red depths of the carving. He stood as one enchanted, seeing ruined civilisations drenched in blood, armadas driven beneath red tides, primal forests devoured by lake-hued flame . . . and lastly he beheld himself in ruin. This latter vision was no imaginary sight, but only a reflection: a one-eyed, scar-faced gargoyle with rotten yellow teeth poking out of receding gums. As he looked at himself in the polished ruby, he wondered if he had always been so ugly, or if the caverns and this castle and his wicked life and diet had made him this way. He had lost all sense of time and did not know his own age, but it seemed impossible that he was as old as his image looked.

With his prize, he descended the stairs, his gait that of an old man. He felt incongruously ancient, but tried to convince himself that he was yet a young boy. Returning to the window overlooking Ausper, he climbed into the round portal, stood in the afternoon sunlight, and began to scream unholy maledictions, holding the bone-and-serpent sceptre above his head.

Far below, one farmer heard a distant shrill and looked up from his hoeing. He saw a tiny, frantic figure in one of the windows of the towers. He dropped his tool and went yelling through the community. Soon there were people at every door looking up at the spectacle of something half-human squealing curses at them. The dry wind became unnaturally still, so that every imprecation reached their ears with full impact, as if the sight alone weren't terrifying enough.

One haggard woman stood in her doorway and thought there was something familiar about the mummy-figure's voice. With sudden dawning, she threw her hands to her mouth and fainted dead away, with no one else in her household to take her in.

Thereafter Ausper suffered plagues, locusts, worse droughts, tornadoes and dust storms. The farmers' livestock suffered every conceivable disease. Children were stillborn. In the years to follow, those who could manage to do so left Ausper with as much of what they owned as could be packed on oxen. A few whose oxen had died tried to escape the town afoot, but these desperate folk had no hope of surviving the waterless plain Those who were unable to flee Ausper resigned themselves to slow, persistent doom.

Eventually those who had remained died of thirst, hunger, illness, or profitless hard work, until there was only one person residing in Ausper. She wandered about the deserted community in her wind-whipped grey robe like a mad hunchbacked beggar, her black sunken eyes darting to and fro in watchful terror.

Unexpectedly, Hode found that he was not exempt from his malicious curses. The same disease that came to kill Ausper's barn fowl killed what birds nested in the cliffs, too. When his once-magnificent eagles were reduced to vultures' lives, pecking in the bones of disease- and drought-killed creatures, the fray-feathered accipitrines were at last overcome by weakness and contagion. One fell into a spiral from the sky, to be broken against the ground. The other toppled from a perch inside the towers.

But over these years, Hode had lost his last measure of humanity. He did not mourn. He had long forgotten the imprecated town and had not bothered to enjoy his vengeance; for revenge, too, was sought for the sake of one of those human emotions of which he had run completely out. In his deafness he never heard the winds his curses brought, much less the pleas of now vanquished peasants who had once prayed for his mercy and made sacrifices at the base of the precipice.

Most of his time had been spent in the labyrinthine caverns beneath the High Place, where he ate of the phantasmagorical gardens and wandered in the complexity of passages. He used his glowing ruby sceptre as a lamp. Too often he chanced upon signs of some intruder, which left slimy trails where it passed. Hode spent months following these tracks over natural bridges, through low tunnels, along narrow ledges, but never caught sight of the presence. The trails inevitably came to places he could not follow, for the being could climb snail-like straight up walls or down chasms.

Sometimes he felt as though he were being egged on by some sort of intelligence, for the slime-trails liked to double back on themselves, or make him follow the most perilous path. He knew it was imperative he find this intruder before it became an intellect greater than his own and a terrible adversary. The thing was obviously growing, for every week it left slightly wider tracks, and was clearing larger sections of fungi on which it foraged with voracious appetite.

So Ausper became a town of ghosts while Hode wandered the caverns. With each passing month and year, he felt himself shrivelling into a prematurely old man. The day came when he was discouraged by his fruitless search and felt too old to carry on. He trudged up from the caverns, kicked aside the bones of his last eagle to die, and leaned against the window ledge. His eye was heavy, his hands weak, his knees shaky. The hand resting upon the sill shook as though palsied, then grew lax and released the ruby sceptre. It rolled from the edge. Hode seemed not to notice. He sighed with the weariness of life.

He took no notice of the bramble-invaded village, nor of the single aged inhabitant wandering about, looting from those who had no more need.

Life had become drudgery. He thought of leaping to his death. He was too tired even to climb over the sill.

His slight frame seemed so heavy that he could hardly stand. He lowered himself to the floor to sit with his back against the wall. Out of the corner of his single eye he caught a motion in the tunnel leading up from the caves. He knew it was the previously elusive creature come to savour its victory. In the dark shadow it could not be made out clearly, but it appeared to be shaped like a man, though its bulk wobbled as though its shape were only tenuous.

Unable or unwilling to move, Hode stared at the watcher in the dark. Likely the being was waiting for night, when it would leap out and devour the passive, indifferent Hode. He could not make himself lay plans for battle. He looked into himself and saw that he was empty and soulless, a man who could spare neither love nor sympathy for friend or family, a wrathful and depraved recluse, feaster of bats and fungi, child-eater, madman without emotion, even a lover of demons.

On this last thought, he jerked his head up and rasped in an ill voice, 'Demon spawn!' He peered at the thing advancing from the shadow. Darkness had fallen. The slavering half-man, half-demon stepped forward, leaving a trail of slime as it dragged what in a travesty sense were feet. It was gelatinous and transparent. By the sharp desert starlight coming through the portals, Hode saw human-like organs within: pulsing heart, pile of rope for intestines, expanding and contracting lungs. The face was rubbery and ever changing, yet in its ugliness Hode saw some familiarity.

Hode did not shout, nor even feel the pain except as a dull burning of no importance, as the half-human thing oozed onto his legs, ingesting his flesh directly into its plasma and by gnawing hunks loose with small, sharp teeth. Hode watched, fascinated, insensitive, as strips of his own hide were ripped away and masticated, and other sections of his body melted as in acid.

While he was eaten and ingested alive, Hode said his final words, addressing the monstrosity enveloping him bit by bit. He said, 'Thou art my heir. Thou art master of the High Place.' Then he was dead, with only the sound of a slobbering feast drifting on the wind from the windows of the High Place where people say no one ever lived.

Paul Ableman lives in London with his wife and small son. A respected author, his novels include *Vac, I Hear Voices* and *Tornado Pratt*. He has also written extensively for the theatre and television and made a name for himself with his controversial treatment of non-fiction subjects: *The Mouth, Anatomy of Nakedness* and *The Doomed Rebellion*.

Daniel the Painter

Paul Ableman

At the age of twenty-five, Daniel West started a furniture business. It flourished and, five years later, he had a chain of nine shops. But then, at the age of thirty, Daniel abruptly decided to become an artist. He sold his business and his luxurious bachelor flat and bought a studio in Chelsea. It was in Mitre Square, that charming patch of grass and shrubs equidistant from the river and the roar of the King's Road. It was large and centrally-heated and included three ancillary rooms and two bathrooms. As soon as he had moved in and decorated the place to his liking, Daniel started to paint. But the results were dismal. When friends, having dutifully inspected some of the products of his easel, asked him why he had abandoned business for art, he usually made a facetious reply.

'Can't waste one's life grinding away at sordid commerce.'
Or
'You probably never suspected that I was a man of refined sensibility.'
Or something equally flippant.

But the truth was that Daniel himself didn't really know why he had changed his entire way of life. It certainly wasn't because he had become disenchanted with business. On the contrary, he loved everything about it and especially watching his bank balance grow. On the other hand, it wasn't because he had long yearned to be a painter. Quite the reverse, he had never felt the smallest desire to paint. He knew very little about art and, although he had sometimes accompanied girlfriends on visits to galleries, he didn't much like looking at pictures. And yet, during his thirtieth year, the impulse to paint had grown stronger and stronger until he could no longer resist it.

For the next five years, Daniel painted a great many bad abstract paintings. He painted in the abstract manner because it was fashionable rather than because it expressed any inner need. From time to time, in the early years, he showed a selection of his paintings to one or the other of the London dealers but none of them showed the slightest interest in his work. Indeed, after a while, some of them began hinting that it would be no disservice to art if he were to abandon his easel. Daniel sold one or two paintings to loyal relatives but, generally speaking, it could hardly be said that he was succeeding in his new career.

Still, he was not unduly depressed.

For one thing, he enjoyed his new life-style. He made a lot of amusing friends in Chelsea and threw a lot of parties. There were often girls hanging about his studio and quite a few of them shared his bed from time to time. Then again, the actual act of painting filled him with a strange, almost breathless, excitement. It was like a tonic or drug. Whenever he started a new picture, he felt a quite unjustifiable conviction of mastery. He felt inspired. But this welcome feeling never survived the completion of the picture. Indeed whenever he contemplated his latest botched effort he would be overcome by something close to despair. But always, at the thought of starting a new picture, the excitement returned.

At the end of five years, Daniel's money gave out. Now, he thought, is the time to chuck it. I've got no more money and, more important, I never did have any talent. I've wasted five years of my life. I'll go back into business.

But he knew that he wouldn't. He was still in the grip of his compulsion to paint. In fact, if anything it was stronger. Almost against his will, he went in search of a new and cheaper studio and, before long, he found one in Clapham. It was much cheaper than the old one and he calculated that, with the proceeds of selling the Chelsea establishment, he should be able to survive for another five years. This was, in fact, a rather daunting prospect because the new studio was very depressing. It was a converted attic in an old, rotting eighteenth-century house in a dismal back street. Many of the other houses in the street were boarded up. Daniel's attic studio was drafty and leaky and its sole facility was a stone sink and a cold-water tap.

Daniel furnished it cheaply and did his best to make it inhabitable. But it was past convincing renovation. He knew that he had

seen the last of his Chelsea friends. They wouldn't troop across
the river to share a bottle of cheap red wine with him in his dank
new premises. The future looked grim. But at the thought of
starting a new painting, his heart beat faster again and the old
thrill of anticipation actually made him tremble. He started work
on his third day in the new studio. He planned the picture
carefully. His blundering progress had by now given him some
insight into things like proportion, colour and harmony. He spent
two days on preliminary sketches and on detailed structural and
chromatic programmes. He had a feeling that if his first painting
in the new studio were a success then his career might still be
redeemed and he would ultimately become an artist. Finally he
took up his palette and brushes and began to work.

He finished the painting three days later. During those days he
had worked almost without a break. Finally he stepped back and
considered his work. It was very different from the amateurish
things he had produced in his early days. The composition was
quite good. The colours were crisp and the harmonies subtle. But
Daniel felt, if anything, an even deeper sense of disappointment.
For the painting was lifeless. It said nothing. It conveyed
nothing. It was pure draughtsmanship. Daniel contemplated it
for quite a long time. Then, almost absently, he took a kitchen
knife and slashed it into ribbons. He deposited the remnants in
the dustbin outside his house. And then he made his way to the
nearest pub where he got very, very drunk.

The next morning Daniel awoke to find, understandably, that
he had a bad headache. He was lying on his back on his divan and
he soon realised that he was fully dressed. He tried to recall what
had happened the previous night. He remembered drinking alone
in the pub but that was all. He had no recollection of leaving the
establishment, walking the hundred yards or so home and then,
presumably, throwing himself onto his bed. He had never before
drunk enough to induce alcoholic amnesia and he was a little
alarmed. Still, apart from the headache, which was already easing
slightly, he seemed in reasonable shape.

After a while, he raised himself gingerly until he was sitting
upright and then, almost immediately, he saw it. It was a painting
and it was resting on his easel. Although the early morning light
was poor and the easel was some distance away he realised at once

that it was not one of his old abstract works. He sat still for some time, gazing at it and then slowly he manoeuvred himself off the bed, crossed the studio and stood in front of it. He swallowed and glanced at the door. No, it wasn't locked. In fact, he hardly ever bothered to push the bolt. That must explain it. It was a practical joke. Someone – perhaps one of his old Chelsea companions – had entered in the night and placed this picture on his easel.

It was an old-fashioned picture. Daniel was no expert on art history but he thought that it was of late nineteenth-century vintage. It was a landscape painting and showed some cows in a field, some trees and a few cottages. It was painted in soft greens and blues and browns. It was clearly a competent piece but, in Daniel's opinion, not a very interesting one. Still, the colours were delicate but vivid and, rather than a hundred years ago, it might almost have been painted –

Daniel gasped and reached forwards and touched the canvas. His finger made a tiny smear. He looked down at his finger and found that there was a trace of umber paint on it. He seized the canvas and carried it to where the light was better. There was no doubt: it was freshly painted. His heart beginning to pound, Daniel carried the picture back to the easel and looked around for his palette. He soon located it on top of his gas-ring and, sure enough, the palette was covered with freshly mixed oil paints that betrayed the tints of the picture itself. Daniel looked down at his clothing. It was free of stains but he saw a corner of dirty cloth emerging from one trouser pocket. He quickly fished out the rag and examined it. It had clearly been used to wipe brushes and the hues were again those of the canvas.

Daniel retreated to his divan and sat down. The conclusion seemed inescapable. He himself had painted the picture. He searched his memory again but he could still recall nothing after drinking in the pub. And yet, if evidence meant anything, he must have come back to the studio and spent the night, or a large part of it, painting this work in a style he had never before attempted and with a degree of competence far beyond anything suggested by his previous efforts.

He rose once more and went to the picture. What did it represent? Was it some scene from his youth? Did it show the neighbourhood of one of his numerous relatives' country houses?

Was it a landscape familiar to him from a childhood holiday? But, strive as he might, he could find no geographical familiarity in the work. Daniel found that he was shivering with a faint, undefined but irrefutable fear.

The next day Daniel took the painting to the Deane Gallery in Bond Street. He had recovered his composure. The work was, after all, his. Just possibly it represented some elaborate hoax but, until that was proved, he was determined to proceed on the assumption that it was his own work. And if he had painted it he might as well see if he could sell it. He had no idea if there was a market for Victorian pastiches but even a few quid would be useful.

Daniel had decided to take the work to the Deane Gallery because this establishment specialised in English landscapes of the eighteenth and nineteenth centuries. Daniel had often passed the place on his way to other galleries and been dissuaded from trying his luck there because his own works were abstract. He doubted if the Deane Gallery, an elegant and clearly prosperous establishment with large windows on Bond Street, would concern itself with his humble effort but perhaps they would direct him to some other gallery that would.

Daniel showed his canvas to a young man who responded to the receptionist's internal telephone call. And, to his surprise, the young man examined the work closely and then, instead of shaking his head with a patronising smile, asked him if he would wait a little while until Mr Deane himself was free. Daniel naturally agreed to do so and, within a quarter of an hour, found himself in a sumptuous office on the second floor where Mr Michael Deane, a grey-haired, red-faced man in his fifties, studied his painting in silence for some time.

'How much?' asked Mr Deane at last, fixing Daniel with a penetrating look.

The question was so unexpected that Daniel merely gaped for a moment. Then he recovered and said quickly:

'How much will you offer me?'

Mr Deane sighed and shook his head. He walked to a window in his office and looked out. Finally, he turned.

'You're not the only one, you know,' he said firmly. 'I can pick up any number of these.'

Mr Deane walked to the picture again and studied it closely. Then he shook his head again but this time with what seemed to be admiration.

'Still I admit you're pretty good. Well, it'll need treatment and a signature and special handling and all the rest – I could manage five-hundred pounds.'

Faintly, Daniel heard his own voice croak.

'How much?'

Deane spoke harshly.

'Don't forget, we take the risk – or most of it. All right, seven-fifty. That's as high as I can go.'

Daniel was neither stupid nor naïve. He realised, even as he strove to grapple with this princely offer, that something dishonest was afoot. The gallery specialised in English landscape. Doubtless Deane was going to sell, or attempt to sell, his picture as a genuine period piece. But what did he care? It was the first time anyone had made him a serious offer for anything he had painted and the amount took his breath away – or most of it. He had just enough left to gasp:

'I'll take it.'

'Good,' purred Deane. 'Good. Well, it's a rising market. Can you do any more?'

Daniel nodded weakly.

'If they are as convincing as this one,' said Deane, 'I'll take them. At the same price. Now, I'll pay you in cash. I don't want to know your name, address, anything about you. When you've got more canvases, telephone and make an appointment. Is that understood?'

Daniel nodded again. Deane bent over the painting suddenly, gasped and murmured:

'You idiot!'

'What is it?' asked Daniel startled.

'You've signed the bloody thing. Why on earth – ? Oh well, I suppose one of my people can get it off but for God's sake don't sign them in future.'

'Of course not,' agreed Daniel humbly.

Ten minutes later, he walked out of the Deane Gallery with seven hundred and fifty pounds in cash in his inside pocket and elation in his heart.

He considered phoning one of his old girlfriends and taking her to lunch at Claridges or the Ritz. But he decided against it. His suit was shabby. Even seven hundred and fifty pounds would not enable him to resume his old affluent life-style. No, the best thing he could do would be to paint a few more of what he had already begun to think of as his 'Victorian' paintings, sell them to Michael Deane and then see about moving back to Chelsea and the life that went with it.

For ten days he toiled at his easel. But his efforts were in vain. He could not get anything right, the figures, the perspective, the colours and especially not the detail. What emerged was a series of muddy canvases in which distorted shapes, reminiscent of a child's attempts to represent nature, loomed absurdly. On the tenth day, he stood gazing at a new, blank canvas for some time. He wanted to start and yet he was terrified of starting. He felt power and inspiration and yet reason told him that, before long, he would be contemplating another disastrous failure. And then suddenly he said aloud a single word:

'Drink.'

He had painted his one good 'Victorian' when he was drunk. Perhaps that was the key. Perhaps he needed the relaxation provided by drink before he could tap the source of inspiration that must be there. He put down his palette and hurried out of the studio. Ten minutes later he returned with five bottles of wine. All afternoon, he drank wine and painted and the painting, which he completed about dusk in a state of advanced drunkenness, was, if anything, worse than the others had been. He had consumed two full bottles of wine and they hadn't helped.

For an hour he lay on his bed contemplating suicide. His good 'Victorian' had clearly been a freak, a sport, something that he couldn't repeat. Probably the painting had been an unconscious copy of some canvas that he had seen as a child and which (he had read of such things) had become indelibly imprinted on his subconscious. He would never do another. He got up and took his kitchen knife. He went to his latest attempt and slashed it to ribbons. Then he opened another bottle of wine and drank it virtually as fast as he could swallow. And then he passed out.

In the morning he knew even before he opened his eyes what he would find. The circumstances were identical. He had a violent headache. He was fully clothed. And he could remember nothing after opening the final bottle of wine. For some time, he didn't even bother to open his eyes and sit up. He simply brooded on his bizarre dilemma. He could, it seemed, paint pastiche master-pieces when he was not merely drunk but paralytic, when he was in a state that should have precluded his even holding a brush, never mind painting with it. He could produce his 'Victorian' paintings in that state and no other. But that state was dangerous. Daniel knew that he couldn't achieve it daily or even weekly and hope to live for very long. Almost dispassionately he reached a conclusion. He would do it once a fortnight. He would drink himself unconscious and paint another 'Victorian'. He would be a 'once-a-fortnight' artist. Having reached this conclusion, he opened his eyes, rose, went to his easel and contemplated the new painting. The scene was comparable to the last one. It showed a field with some horses, a manor house and a meandering stream. It was wrought in the same staple blues, greens and browns but this time there were hints of crimson and yellow. It was, of its kind, a wonderful thing. Daniel peered at the right-hand corner. There was his signature. Thoughtfully, he took up his palette and a brush and carefully painted it out. He smiled grimly at the thought that the only part of the work that he could do consciously was to remove something from it.

That afternoon, after a profitable visit to the Deane Gallery, he returned to Chelsea and started looking for a studio. Naturally, he first tried to obtain his old one again but it was not available. Before long, however, he found another one that was quite as comfortable and nearly as attractive. The next day he moved in.

For the next three years, Daniel was a 'once-a-fortnight' painter. For the rest of the time he simply amused himself. The old gang flocked back to his studio. He had all the girls he wanted and as much company as he pleased. But, on each alternate Wednesday, he cleared everyone out of the studio, locked and bolted the door and drank himself insensible. And the next morning a new 'Victorian' gleamed on his easel. By now, Michael Deane was paying him two-thousand pounds in cash for each of them. Daniel was a wealthy young man but he was not really happy. His nocturnal feats offered him no sense of achievement and their clandestine sale denied him any acclaim. He made sporadic resolves to abandon painting and return to the honest work of business but the ease with which he secured a handsome living kept him tied to his strange routine.

One evening Daniel's current girl-friend, a debutante called Jill, offered to take him to a party. The host, it seemed, was a wealthy young peer. The peer's home, Jill explained, was a very grand house in Belgravia. Daniel went to many parties and was rather bored with them. But, as usual, he had nothing better to do and so, on the appointed night, he drove Jill and himself to Belgravia in his green Mercedes.

No sooner had the couple been ushered into a large, thronged drawing room where servants were drifting about with trays of canapes and drinks than Daniel stopped dead. On the wall facing him, in a splendid gold frame and with its own individual light above it, was a painting. It showed a shepherd followed by his dog wending his way down a slope towards a village. In the background a sunset blazed through a copse on a hilltop. As if in a trance, Daniel strode across the room and stood gazing up at the painting. Before long, he heard a masculine voice close to his ear. He turned and found that a young man was smiling at him. Having missed what the young man had said, Daniel murmured:

'I'm sorry?'

The other spoke again.

'I simply asked if you were a Tomkins enthusiast?'

'Tomkins?' echoed Daniel without comprehension. He saw Jill, just behind the young man, gesturing meaningfully and realised that he was being addressed by Lord Rainley, their host. The young peer nodded.

'You made a beeline for it. There are one or two quite decent things in the house but that's the prize package. It's a Beech Hill Tomkins, you know.'

Daniel shook his head apologetically.

'I don't I'm afraid.'

The other frowned.

'But Jill's just told me that you're a painter. Are you saying that you've never heard of Daniel Tomkins?'

'Never.'

'Oh well – how about a drink?'

'Fine. But I am interested – who's Daniel Tomkins?'

'Hardly the moment for a seminar, old boy.'

'True but – couldn't you just give me the basic facts? I'm – terribly impressed by this painting.'

Lord Rainley glanced about the room as if in search of social obligations. Then he smiled aimiably.

'Come on, we'll pop into the library for a minute.'

Once seated in the small but well-stocked library, Lord Rainley told Daniel something about Daniel Tomkins. It seemed he was a Victorian landscape painter who, during his lifetime, had enjoyed small success. He had lived and worked in London until he was twenty-eight and then poverty had driven him out. He spent the last two years of his life in the village of Beech Hill in Kent. And the work he did at Beech Hill was now regarded as his finest.

'And I gather he's become very famous?' prompted Daniel.

Lord Rainley made an amused gesture.

'Good Lord, yes. He's considered – rightly, in my opinion – the finest exponent of the English landscape school.'

'And he was poor all his life?'

'Such as it was. He drank himself to death when he was thirty.'

A cold shiver went through Daniel. He had been thirty when he had first felt an irresistible compulsion to paint. A moment later he said:

'Did you get it at the Deane Gallery? Sort of thing they specialise in.'

'Yes, Deane found it for me.'

Daniel hadn't just guessed at the picture's provenance. He knew something that Lord Rainley didn't. He knew that the picture on the wall of the Belgravia house was not a Beech Hill Daniel Tomkins. It was actually a Chelsea Daniel West. Daniel West had painted it only a few months before. It had been artificially aged. It had been given a craquelure and the colours had been slightly dulled as if by old varnish. It had also been given a very faint signature, almost illegible but certainly not Daniel West's.

There was only one more important fact that Daniel West wanted to know. He smiled diffidently.

'Way out of my reach, I'm sure,' he ventured. 'But – how much would a painting like that cost?'

Lord Rainley looked a little smug.

'I paid thirty-seven thousand – which is nothing for a Beech Hill Tomkins. And now I think I'll have to get back to my mob, old boy. Come along and collar a drink.'

With the astounding sum echoing in his head, Daniel followed his host back into the drawing room.

At 8 a.m. the next day, Daniel was humming along the Brighton motorway at a steady seventy miles an hour. He had not looked up the location of Beech Hill in his road atlas. Lord Rainley had mentioned that it was in Kent but that was all the information Daniel had. And yet he never hesitated. At the final motorway exit, at Pease Pottage, he turned off the motorway and drove a further eighteen or so miles through twisting country lanes. And when he finally drew up outside a little gem of an Early English parish church, he knew without having seen any sign-posts, that he was in the village of Beech Hill.

Many of the cottages had been modernised. They had garages attached to them, television aerials on their roofs and cars parked outside but essentially the village was unspoilt. It was quite a large village, given additional spread by a large, willow-fringed duck-pond set in a broad green. It had a general purpose shop that doubled as a post office but no other sign of commerce. Daniel, however, devoted no time to sightseeing. As soon as he had climbed out of his Mercedes he set off up a narrow side street. Soon he had left the village behind and, about a half mile beyond it, he turned off what had become a country lane onto a desig-nated Public Footpath. He followed this winding trail through delightful vistas of low bluffs, meadows and little woods for some two miles further and then he climbed through a sagging barbed wire fence into a sloping field. There he stopped and gazed.

Below him were a few cottages. In the meadow across which he observed them were three or four ancient trees of noble size and around them cows grazed on the still damp grass.

For a long time Daniel stared at this tranquil scene. He already knew it. Indeed, he had painted it. It was the site of his first 'Victorian' painting which, he now knew, had been executed to perfection in the style of a long-dead landscape painter whose existence he had never even heard of until the previous day.

Daniel turned and retraced his steps to the footpath. He followed it for a while and then struck out through an almost pathless little wood. Emerging from the trees, he stopped once more. Ahead of him was the scene of his second 'Victorian': a manor house on a hillside, a little stream, even some horses. Again Daniel gazed and marvelled while a dread he wanted urgently to suppress slowly gathered strength.

All that day, Daniel strode through the countryside surrounding the lovely village of Beech Hill, visiting scenes that he had never seen before but which, during nights when he had been insensible with drink, he had reproduced magnificently on canvas. At about six that evening, he returned to the village. Again without any hesitation, he walked along a narrow street until he reached the last cottage on his left. He rang the doorbell. There was quite a long pause and then a white-haired crone, whose rheumatic shuffle he had heard slowly approaching, opened the door. She eyed him listlessly for a moment and then muttered:

'Tomkins?'

Daniel merely nodded in reply.

'You're the third one this year,' the woman grumbled. 'It's hard. I don't get paid for showing it, you know. The Council keep bringing it up and saying I should get a proper salary but nothing ever comes of it.'

Daniel took out his wallet and handed the woman a ten-pound note. Her grumbling ceased.

'It's upstairs,' she said. 'But there's nothing much to see. You go first. I'm so slow. It's the door facing you at the top.'

Daniel hurried up the stairs, raised the wooden latch of the door opposite the stairhead and entered a tiny room. There was indeed very little to see, only a wooden bed and a wooden table and chair. But Daniel felt his whole body tingling as if a mild electric shock were passing through it. He heard the old lady's voice behind him.

'He lived in this room and he died in it. And that's all there is. None of his paintings. Just the one my grandmother did of him.'

At these words, Daniel walked swiftly across the little chamber to the table. He pulled open a drawer at one end and removed from it a small, framed picture. He heard a faint gasp of surprise from behind him.

'How did you know where it was?'

Daniel made no reply. She resumed:

'I keep it in there to keep off the light. They say light's bad for it. Of course, my grandmother wasn't an artist. But it looks like him. Them as knows says it's a good likeness.'

Daniel stared at the face on the picture. The old woman shuffled across the room and peered over his arm.

'Well, I never,' she said. 'You look like him.'

'A little,' returned Daniel softly. 'Just a little.'

But it was not true. It wasn't just a little. The resemblance was uncanny. Daniel West's face was a little heavier than that on the portrait. But then Daniel West was now approaching forty. At thirty he had been virtually the double of Daniel Tomkins.

It was dark when Daniel drove back to London. As he drove, he repeated to himself: is that all? I look like him and I've got the same first name? Is that all?

Daniel repeated it like an incantation. It helped to keep him from thinking too deeply about the web of displaced time and longing in which he had become enmeshed. He didn't want to recognise that he was somehow fulfilling the truncated ambitions of a long-dead artist. He had always been a rational young man, contemptuous of the supernatural, and he refused even now to acknowledge openly what he had secretly known for a long time; he, Daniel West, supplied only the physical energy for painting his 'Victorians'. Another's spirit guided his brush.

As Daniel began to glide gratefully through the lighted streets that signified the outskirts of London, he tried to concentrate on the beckoning charms of his Chelsea studio. He had several friends staying and he knew that, once he had arrived home, there would be food and wine and laughter, not the sort of ambience in which thwarted phantoms thrive. Tomorrow he would destroy all his artist's equipment and then he would see about resuming his career as a businessman. And he would never, as long as he lived, pass again within twenty miles of the lovely village of Beech Hill where a man had once lived whose desire to paint had been stronger than the grave.

The traffic was light and, some twenty minutes later, Daniel pulled up outside his studio and swung quickly out of his car. He had only taken a few steps when he stopped dead. He was not in Chelsea. He felt a thrill of near panic as he glanced about and saw rotting, boarded-up façades on both sides of the street. His car, not his volition, had brought him to Clapham and to his old, derelict studio. He turned with the intention of throwing himself back into the Mercedes and fleeing. Then he paused – and turned back again. Aware that he was shivering violently, he gazed through the gloom, dimly lit by the old-fashioned street lights, at the leprous façade of the house. It was somehow different. It was not quite the same as it had been when he had occupied its mouldering attic and painted the posthumous works of Daniel Tomkins there. But what was the difference? Daniel knew that he had to find out. Fighting his dread he pushed open the wrought-iron gate and advanced up the short path. The house was dark and obviously untenanted. But the street light gave just enough illumination to show Daniel what he sought. And as he realised what it was, his fear wondrously dissolved. He understood that what he was seeing represented, for him, a message of farewell. His task was over. He was free again. Slowly he read the bold words on the plaque that must have been recently installed above the front door by the pious guardians of London's historic past: GREATER LONDON COUNCIL – DANIEL TOMKINS 1869–1899 – PAINTER – LIVED HERE.

Rachel Pollack is an American author who lives in Amsterdam where she writes and manages a bookshop. Her two novels are *Golden Vanity* and *The Country of the Dead* and she has written books on the Tarot. Her story is a fascinating attempt at creating a modern form of fairy tale.

The Girl who Went to the Rich Neighbourhood

Rachel Pollack

There was once a widow who lived with her six daughters in the poorest neighbourhood in town. In summer the girls all went barefoot, and even in winter they often had to pass one pair of shoes between them as they ran through the street. Even though the mother got a cheque every month from the welfare department, it never came to enough, despite their all eating as little as possible. They would not have survived at all if the supermarkets hadn't allowed the children to gather behind the loading gates at the end of the day and collect the crushed or fallen vegetables.

Sometimes, when there was no more money, the mother would leave her left leg as credit with the grocer. When her cheque came, or one of the children found a little work, she would get back her leg and be able to walk without the crutch her oldest daughter had made from a splintery board. One day, however, after she'd paid her bill, she found herself stumbling. When she examined her leg she discovered that the grocery had kept so many legs and arms jumbled together in their big metal cabinet that her foot had become all twisted. She sat down on their only chair and began to cry, waving her arms over her head.

Seeing her mother so unhappy the youngest girl, whose name was Rose, walked up and announced, 'Please don't worry. I'll go to the rich neighbourhood.' Her mother kept crying. 'And I'll speak to the mayor. I'll get him to help us.' The widow smiled and stroked her daughter's hair.

She doesn't believe me, Rose thought. Maybe she won't let me go. I'd better sneak away. The next day, when the time came to go to the supermarket Rose took the shoes she shared with her sisters and slipped them in her shopping bag. She hated doing this, but she would need the shoes for the long walk to the rich neighbourhood. Besides, maybe the mayor wouldn't see her if she came barefoot. Soon, she told herself, she'd bring back shoes for everyone. At the supermarket she filled her bag with seven radishes that had fallen off the bunch, two sticks of yellowed celery, and four half-blackened bananas. Well, she thought, I guess I'd better get started.

As soon as she left the poor neighbourhood Rose saw some boys shoving and poking a weak old lady who was trying to cross the street. What a rotten thing to do, the girl thought, and hoped the children in the rich neighbourhood weren't all like that. She found a piece of pipe in the street and chased them away.

'Thank you,' wheezed the old woman, who wore a yellow dress and had long blonde hair that hung, uncombed, down to her knees. She sat down in the middle of the road, with cars going by on every side. Rose said, 'Shouldn't we get out of the street? We could sit on the pavement.'

'I can't,' said the old woman, 'I must eat something first. Don't you have anything to eat?'

Rose reached in her basket to give the old woman a radish. In a moment the shrivelled red thing had vanished and the woman held out her hand. Rose gave her another radish, and then another, until all the radishes had slid down the old woman's densely veined throat. 'Now we can go,' she said, and instantly jumped to her feet to drag Rose across the road.

Rose told herself that maybe she wouldn't need them. She looked down at the silver pavement and then up at the buildings that reached so far above her head the people in the windows looked like toys. 'Is this the rich neighbourhood?' she asked.

'Hardly,' the woman said, 'you have to go a long way to reach the rich neighbourhood.' Rose thought how she'd better be extra careful with the rest of her food. The old woman said, 'But if you really want to go there I can give you something to help you.' She ran her fingers through her tangled gold hair and when she took them out she was holding a lumpy yellow coin. 'This token will always get you on or off the underground railway.'

What a strange idea, thought Rose. How could you use a token more than once? And even if you could, everyone knew that you didn't need anything to get off the underground. But she put the coin in the bag and thanked the old woman.

All day she walked and when night came she crawled under a fire escape beside some cardboard cartons. She was very hungry but she thought she had better save her celery and bananas for the next day. Trying not to think of the warm mattress she shared with two of her sisters, she went to sleep.

The next morning the sound of people marching to work woke her up. She stretched herself, thinking how silver streets may look very nice but didn't made much of a bed. Then she rubbed her belly and stared at the celery. I'd better get started first, she told herself. But when she began to walk her feet hurt, for her sisters' shoes, much too big for her, had rubbed the skin raw the day before.

Maybe she could take the tube train. Maybe the old woman's token would work at least once. She went down a subway entrance where a guard with a gun walked back and forth, sometimes clapping his hands or stamping his feet. As casually as she could Rose walked up and put her token in the slot. I hope he doesn't shoot me, she thought. But then the wooden blades of the gate turned and she passed through.

A moment later, she was walking down the stairs when she heard a soft clinking sound. She turned around to see the token bouncing on its rim along the corridor and down the stairs until it bounced right into the shopping bag. Rose looked to see if the guard was taking his gun out but he was busy staring out the entrance.

All day she travelled on the tube train, but whenever she tried to read the signs she couldn't make out what they said beneath the huge black marks drawn all over them. Rose wondered if the marks formed the magic that made the trains go. She'd sometimes heard people say that without magic the underground would break down forever. Finally she decided she must have reached the rich neighbourhood. She got off the train, half expecting to have to use her token. But the exit door swung open with no trouble and soon she found herself on a gold pavement, with buildings that reached so high the people looked like birds fluttering around in giant caves.

Rose was about to ask someone for the mayor's office when she saw a policeman with a gold mask covering his face slap an old woman. Rose hid in a doorway and made a sound like a siren, a trick she'd learned in the poor neighbourhood. The policeman ran off waving his gold truncheon.

'Thank you, thank you,' said the old woman whose tangled red hair reached down to her ankles. 'I'm so hungry now, could you give me something to eat?' Trying not to cry Rose gave the woman first one piece of celery and then the other. Then she asked, 'Is this the rich neighbourhood?'

'No, no, no,' the woman laughed, 'but if you're planning to go there I can give you something that might help you.' She ran her fingers through her hair and took out a red feather. 'If you need to reach something and cannot, then wave this feather.' Rose couldn't imagine how a feather could help her reach anything but she didn't want to sound rude so she put the feather in her bag.

Since it was evening and Rose knew that gangs sometimes ran through the streets after dark she thought she'd better find a place to sleep. She saw a pile of wooden crates in front of a store and lay down behind them, sadly thinking how she'd better save her four bananas for the next day.

The next morning the sound of opening and closing car doors woke her up, and she stretched painfully. The gold streets had hurt her back even more than the silver ones the night before. With a look at her bananas, now completely black, she got to her feet and walked back to the underground.

All day she rode on the train, past underground store windows showing clothes that would tear in a day, and bright flimsy furniture, and strange machines with rows of black buttons. The air became very sweet, but thick, as if someone had sprayed the tunnels with perfume. Finally Rose decided she couldn't breathe and had to get out.

She came up to a street made all of diamond, and buildings so high she couldn't see anything at all in the windows, only flashes of colours. The people walking glided a few inches above the ground, while the cars moved so gently on their white tyres they looked like swimmers floating in a pool.

Rose was about to ask for the mayor's office when she saw an old woman surrounded by manicured dogs and rainbow dyed cats whose rich owners had let them roam the street. Rose whistled so high she herself couldn't hear it, but the animals all ran away, thinking their owners had called them for dinner.

'Thank you *so* much,' the woman said, dusting off her long black dress. Her black hair trailed the ground behind her. 'Do you suppose you could give me something to eat?'

Biting back her tears Rose held out the four bananas. The woman laughed and said, 'One is more than enough for me. You eat the others.' Rose had to stop herself shoving all three bananas into her mouth at once. She was glad she did, for each one tasted like a different food, from chicken to strawberries. She looked up amazed.

'Now,' said the woman, 'I suppose you want the mayor's house.' Her mouth open, Rose nodded yes. The woman told her to look for a street so bright she had to cover her eyes to walk on it. Then she said, 'If you ever find the road too crowded blow on this.' She ran her fingers through her hair and took out a black whistle shaped like a pigeon. The girl said 'Thank you,' though she didn't think people would get out of the street just for a whistle.

When the woman had gone Rose looked around at the diamond street. I'd break my back sleeping here, she thought, and decided to look for the mayor's house that evening. Up and down the streets she hobbled, now and then running out of the way of dark-windowed cars or lines of children dressed all in money and holding hands as they ran screaming through the street.

At one point she saw a great glow of light and thought she must have found the mayor's house, but when she came close she saw only an empty road where bright balls of light on platinum poles shone on giant fountains spouting liquid gold into the air. Rose shook her head and walked on.

Several times she asked people for the mayor's house but no one seemed to hear or see her. As night came Rose thought that at least the rich neighbourhood wouldn't get too cold; they probably heated the streets. But instead of warm air a blast of cold came up from the damned pavement. The people in the rich neighbourhood chilled the streets so they could use the personal heaters built into their clothes.

For the first time Rose thought she would give up. It was all so strange, how could she ever think the mayor would even listen to her? About to look for a subway entrance she saw a flash of light a few blocks away and began to walk towards it. When she came close the light became so bright she automatically covered her eyes, only to find she could see just as well as before. Scared now that she'd actually found the mayor she slid forward close to the buildings.

The light came from a small star which the mayor's staff had captured and set in a lead cage high above the street. A party was going on, with people dressed in all sorts of costumes. Some looked like birds with beaks instead of noses, and giant feathered wings growing out of their backs; other had become lizards, their heads covered in green scales. In the middle, on a huge chair of black stone sat the mayor looking very small in a white fur robe. Long curved fingernails hooked over the ends of his chair. All around him advisers floated in the air on glittery cushions.

For a time Rose stayed against the wall, afraid to move. Finally she told herself she could starve just standing there. Trying not to limp, she marched forward and said, 'Excuse me.'

No one paid any attention. And no wonder. Suspended from a helicopter a band played on peculiar horns and boxes. 'Excuse me,' Rose said louder, then shouted, the way she'd learned to shout in the poor neighbourhood when animals from outside the city attacked the children.

Everything stopped. The music sputtered out, the lizards stopped snatching at the birds who stopped dropping jewelled 'eggs' on the lizards' heads. Two policemen ran forward. Masks like smooth mirrors covered their heads so that the rich people would only see themselves if they happened to glance at a policeman. They grabbed Rose's arms, but before they could handcuff her the mayor boomed (his voice came through a microphone grafted onto his tongue), 'Who are you? What do you want? Did you come to join the party?'

Everyone laughed. Even in the rich neighbourhood, they knew, you had to wait years for an invitation to the mayor's party.

'No sir,' said Rose. 'I came to ask for help for the poor neighbourhood. Nobody has any money to buy food and people have to leave their arms and legs at the grocery just to get anything. Can you help us?'

The laughter became a roar. People shouted ways the mayor could help the poor neighbourhood. Someone suggested canning the ragged child and sending her back as charity dinners. The mayor held up his hand and everyone became silent. 'We could possibly help you,' he said. 'But first you will have to prove yourself. Will you do that?'

Confused, Rose said yes. She didn't know what he meant. She wondered if she needed a welfare slip or some other identification. 'Good,' the mayor said. 'We've got a small problem here and maybe you could help us solve it.' He waved a hand and a picture appeared in the air in front of Rose. She saw a narrow metal stick about a foot long with a black knob at one end and a white knob at the other. The mayor told Rose that the stick symbolised the mayor's power, but the witches had stolen it.

'Why don't you send the police to get it back?' Rose asked. Again the mayor had to put up his hand to stop the laughter. He told the girl that the witches had taken the stick to their embassy near the United Nations, where diplomatic immunity kept the police from following them.

'I have to go to the witches' embassy?' Rose asked. 'I don't even know where it is. How will I find it?' But the mayor paid no attention to her. The music started and the birds and lizards went back to chasing each other.

Rose was walking away when a bird woman flapped down in front of her. 'Shall I tell you the way to the witches' embassy?' 'Yes,' Rose said, 'Please.' The woman bent over laughing. Rose thought she would just fly away again, but no, in between giggles she told the girl exactly how to find the witches. Then she wobbled away on her wingtips, laughing so hard she bumped into buildings whenever she tried to fly.

With her underground token Rose arrived at the embassy in only a few minutes. The iron door was so tall she couldn't even reach the bell, so she walked around looking for a servants' entrance. Shouts came from an open window. She crept forward.

Wearing nothing but brown oily mud all over their bodies the witches were dancing before a weak fire. The whole embassy house smelled of damp moss. Rose was about to slip away when she noticed a charred wooden table near the window, and on top of it the mayor's stick.

She was about to climb over the sill, grab the stick and run, when she noticed little alarm wires strung across the bottom of the window. Carefully she reached in above the wires towards the table. No use. The stick lay a good six inches out of reach.

An image of the woman in red came to her. 'If you need to reach something and cannot, then wave this feather.' Though she still couldn't see how the feather could help her, especially with something so heavy, she fluttered it towards the table.

The red-haired woman appeared behind the witches, who nevertheless seemed not to notice her. 'I am the East Wind,' she said, and Rose saw that her weakness had vanished and her face shone as bright as her hair waving behind her. 'Because you helped me and gave me your food when you had so little I will give you what you want.' She blew on the table and a gust of wind carried the stick over the wires into Rose's hands.

The girl ran off with all the speed she'd learned running away from trouble in the poor neighbourhood. Before she could go half a block, however, the stick cried out, 'Mistresses! This little one is stealing me.'

In an instant the witches were after her, shrieking and waving their arms as they ran, leaving drops of mud behind them. Soon, however, Rose reached the underground where her token let her inside while the witches, who hadn't taken any money, let alone tokens, could only stand on the other side of the gate and scream at her.

Rose could hardly sit she was so excited. The tube train clacked along, and only the silly weeping of the stick in her bag kept her from jumping up and down. She imagined her mother's face when she came home in the mayor's car piled so high with money and food.

At the stop for the mayor's house Rose stepped off the train swinging her bag. There, lined up across the exit, stood the witches. They waved their muddy arms and sang peculiar words in warbly high pitched voices. The stick called, 'Mistresses, you found me.'

Rose looked over her shoulder at the underground. She could run back, but suppose they were waiting for her in the tunnel? And she still had to get to the mayor. Suddenly she remembered the old woman saying that the token could get her off the underground as well as on. She grabbed it from her bag and held it up.

The woman in yellow appeared before her. 'I am the South Wind,' she said, 'and because you helped me I will help you.' Gently she blew on Rose and a wind as soft as an old bed carried the girl over the heads of the witches and right out of the underground to the street.

As fast as she could she ran to the mayor's house. But as soon as she turned the corner to the street with the captured star she stopped and clutched her bag against her chest. The mayor was waiting for her, wrapped in a head to toe cylinder of bullet-proof glass, while behind him, filling the whole street, stood a giant squad of police. Their mirrored heads bounced the starlight back to the sky. 'Give me the witches' stick,' the mayor said.

'The witches? You said –'

'Idiot child. That stick contains the magic of the witches' grandmothers.' He then began to rave about smashing the witches' house and putting them to work in the power stations underneath the rich neighbourhood. Rose tried to back away. 'Arrest her,' the mayor said.

What had the old woman in black said? 'If you ever find the road too crowded, blow on this.' Rose grabbed the pigeon whistle and blew as hard as she could. The woman appeared, her hair wider than the whole wave of police. 'I am the North Wind,' she told the girl, and might have said more but the squad was advancing. The North Wind threw out her arms and instead of a gust of air a huge flock of black pigeons flew from her dress to pick up the mayor and all the police. Ferociously beating their wings the pigeons carried them straight over the wall into the Northern Borough, where they were captured by burglars and never heard from again.

'Thank you,' Rose said, but the old woman was gone. With a sigh Rose took out the witches' stick. 'I'm sorry,' she told it. 'I just wanted to help the poor neighbourhood.'

'May I go home now?' the stick asked sarcastically. Before the girl could answer the stick sprang out of her hands and flew end over end through the air, back to the witches' embassy.

Rose found herself limping along the riverside, wondering what she would tell her mother and her sisters. Why didn't I help the West Wind? she said to herself. Maybe she could've done something for me.

A woman all in silver appeared on the water. Her silver hair tumbled behind her into the river. 'I do not need to test you to know your goodness,' she said. She blew on the river and a large wave rose up to drench the surprised girl.

But when Rose shook the water off she found that every drop had become a jewel. Red, blue, purple, green, stones of all shapes and colours, sapphires in the shape of butterflies, opals with sleeping faces embedded in the centre, they all covered Rose's feet up to her ankles. She didn't stop to look at them. With both hands she scooped them up into her basket, and then her shoes. Hurry, she told herself. She knew that no matter how many police you got rid of there were always more. And wouldn't the rich people insist the jewels belonged to them?

So full of jewels she could hardly run Rose waddled to the underground entrance. Only when she got there did she notice that the streets had lost their diamond paving. All around her the rich people stumbled or fell on the lumpy grey concrete. Some of them had begun to cry or to crawl on all fours, feeling the ground like blind people at the edge of a cliff. One woman had taken off all her clothes, her furs and silks and laces, and was spreading them all about the ground to hide its ugliness.

Fascinated, Rose took a step back towards the street. She wondered if anything had happened to the star imprisoned in its cage above the mayor's house. But then she remembered how her mother had limped when the grocer had gotten her foot all twisted. She ran downstairs to use her magic token for the last time.

Though the tube train was crowded Rose found a seat in the corner where she could bend over her treasures to hide them from any suspicious eyes. What does a tax collector look like, she wondered.

As the rusty wheels of the train shrieked through the gold neighbourhood and then the silver one Rose wondered if she'd ever see the old ladies again. She sighed happily. It didn't matter. She was going home, back to her mother and her sisters and all her friends in the poor neighbourhood.

The following story is an ambiguous blend of SF archetypes, fantasy and sexual fantasies of a rather gentle nature. Maxim Jakubowski, apart from compiling the *Lands of Never* anthologies, is a London publisher active in many fields: music (*The Rock Yearbook, The Wit and Wisdom of Rock and Roll, The Rock Album*), SF and fantasy (*The Complete Book of SF and Fantasy Lists, Twenty Houses of the Zodiac*). His next two projects are an Encyclopedia of Fantasy (for Allen & Unwin) and a biography of American author Philip K. Dick. He is partial to female images.

Oblique Strategies

Maxim Jakubowski

It was one of those summers when women went topless on foreign beaches. He'd never been a 'tit man' but the idea of hundreds or even thousands of bare, ripe breasts of all shapes and sizes out there under the sun obsessed him like nothing had done before.

He would dream of all the girls he had never had, those he had worshipped from afar, those whose hands he had held (are my palms sweaty?) briefly before they had refused further contact, those who lived with other men and unknowingly broke his heart. He would think of them endlessly as the summer days persistently peeled away like snake skin never to return again.

But, most of all, he would daydream of Agnetha Eklander, who three years before had changed his airline ticket in a travel agency in Kristiansand, Norway. At most, he had spent ten or fifteen minutes in her presence while she checked up on the ticket on her computer terminal display and then rewrote it. He had spent all that time watching her in what he considered his most seductive and brazen manner, with a sort of come hither suave smile whenever she looked up briefly from her desk. Agnetha Eklander. It might not even have been her own name. Perhaps she was deputising for the real Agnetha during the lunch break, this captivating girl with blonde hair, eyes of blue and high cheek-bones. In all honesty she wasn't even particularly pretty. But like all the women who catch your attention, there was something special, the curve of her lips, the shape of her chin, the way her hair was drawn back, that shot through his innards like an arrow.

Awopbopaloobopalopbamboom went the tightened muscles in his stomach and he knew instantly that he would never forget Agnetha Eklander again. Ever. She spoke English with a curious accent, but he felt too self-conscious to start a conversation beyond the banalities of air flight calculations and tariffs and the presence of the gruff, older local agent of his company who was driving him on this business trip intimidated him anyway. Shortly after they'd left the travel agents and taken the route to the local brewery where they had an appointment to discuss the use of hop concentrates, he'd furtively written her name down on his pad of sales reports and sworn to himself that one day he'd return to Kristiansand and get to know her.

He left Norway the next day and had never had the opportunity to return since.

And, today, he sat fantasising wildly about the uncovered breasts of Agnetha Eklander. Wondering how they would feel under his exploring fingers and what shade of pink her nipples would be as they grew imperceptibly harder under a man's fleeting caress. The daily newspapers and his wife's fashion magazines extolled the pleasures and virtues of topless sunbathing and he would imagine in turn the texture of the grains of sand on an Italian or French beach rippling down the valley separating Agnetha's tanned breasts as she stood up to face the sea, and the sand flowed down towards her sex.

Jake closed his eyes and sighed.

Downstairs, the children were quarrelling again. The children always seemed to be quarrelling.

Summer was almost over already and, yet again, he'd missed out the far beaches of a thousand and one nipples. Everything felt wrong.

'I'm just going out to get some cigarettes,' he called out to his wife, as he walked out of the house towards the car.

'But you don't smoke,' she answered back from the open kitchen window, thinking it was just another of his jokes.

'I'll be back soon,' he said and drove off.

Three and a half days later he reached Rainbow Alley and found a room at the Newsky Prospekt Hotel. It was the end of the holiday season and tourists, mostly German families with heavy-built Mercedes and Opel cars with roofracks, were deserting the resort in droves. The sea was turning grey and even the sun seemed strangely hesitant when making early morning appearances.

'We're the only place to remain open throughout the year,' the receptionist told Jake as he signed the register book. 'Many people like you enjoy the out-of-season days. There's less of a crowd. That'll be fifty dollars in advance, sir.'

Jake handed over his American Express card.

'Have a happy day.'

On the beach, the few women still young enough to wear bikinis all wore tops.

As autumn dragged along, days getting shorter and the nearby beach increasingly deserted of holidaymakers, Jake gradually met the other inhabitants of the hotel.

'Length of stay indeterminate,' said Hugo in the dimly lit bar.

'And I'm leaving for home tomorrow,' revealed his dark-haired, plumpish girlfriend Ingrid with a quizzical smile as she looked towards Hugo, perhaps seeking some kind of reaction. He remained impassive.

'And he's the barman,' continued Ingrid, pointing at the balding guy hunched behind the counter.

'Indeed, I'm the barman. No need for a name. Just call me "barman" and I'll serve you a drink. Any drink,' he said, winking at Jake knowingly. Which puzzled Jake who never touched alcohol.

'As she's hopping off to suburbia, would you consider sharing a room with me? It would be cheaper for both of us. Especially if you're staying the winter,' Hugo suggested.

'Not a bad idea,' Jake answered. 'If it's all right with you?'

'Sure. And I don't snore at night.'

'I can vouch for that,' said Ingrid, ordering another round.

'And we can play the Waiting Game,' Hugo added. 'It can really be great fun.'

'Sounds great,' Jake nodded. 'I've never played it before. But I've heard a lot about it.'

Quiet winter evenings. Over in the hills that dominate the shoreline, dogs howl at night and sullen owls rhythmically sing songs of woe. An out of this world rock concert. When it rains, the beach changes colour.

Behind the clean, geometrical curtains drawn over the window overlooking the sea, they sit for hours on end watching the sinuous road spiral down towards the sea. In silence, maybe trying to imagine the sounds of faraway outside, where giant waves break in grand fashion against the fragrant barrier of the coast.

In days of old, when hardy pirates sailed the seas, learned cartographers had called the peninsula 'Desolation Row'. Truth is, the silhouette of the land seen from out at sea is dull and featureless and offers no invitation to wandering minds.

They wait.

The moving shadows on the marine horizon, the whirling birds flying an old-fashioned tango pattern around the telegraph poles, the empty sky, the landscape. Sometimes, Jake has the feeling that they have somehow become embedded into the landscape: sentient micro-dots dropped at random within the impressionistic painting of some godlike amateur artist who, for good measure, has left his work unfinished.

On the other side of the hotel, in another room facing the bay, Ingrid and the barman also wait. A flicker of light from the tip of a cigarette as darkness tucks the night in and the ocean dozes off. Above Rainbow Alley, the mirror of time controls destinies.

That's what Jake and Hugo call it: the mirror of time. It's not really a mirror, you can't see anything in it. Seen through their binoculars it's just an anonymous patch of sky, a bit foggy, nebulous and hazy. Right now, the principle of the game is to imagine that it might be a hole in time or space, a tear in the space-time continuum, just like in a science-fiction story full of hoary old clichés. One day, very soon maybe, someone or something might appear through it and drop down into the sea below. A worn-out boot, a bicycle wheel, the ghost of Amelia Earhart, Judge Crater, Ambrose Bierce or the full complement of the Marie Celeste. Fine hopes.

Back in the other room, the barman and Ingrid (who had finally decided not to return to her native city after all – what is there to life behind a desk?) have conceived another clever game model. They are waiting to devise an expedition to explore what lies on the other side of death. It's not what exists beyond that fascinates them so, but the complications of the journey. Suicides in awesome synchronisation, ultimate shared orgasms to bridge the gap between now and there? The precise method is still being sought.

At the window, Jake daydreams while Hugo lying fully clothed on the bed leafs through a stroke magazine. He misses his wife, he misses his children and cannot now for the life of him understand why he took off so suddenly. He hasn't had the guts to phone them; it's been a few weeks already. They will by now have given up on him. It's not that he doesn't love them, but something snapped, this god-awful feeling that 'is life all there is to living?' and was genteel happiness enough. Wasn't he missing out on something dreadfully important?

Jake thinks about Agnetha Eklander. Tries to imagine the smell of her body. The perfume of the sweat pearling down her sides under the fiery sun of an exotic beach. The smell of her crotch before and after love. The garlic-tinged breath surrounding her as she walks bare-breasted to the bathroom to wash her teeth before joining him in bed. The aroma of her clothes scattered across the chairs and the jute carpeting.

'Oh, shit!' he snaps out of his moodiness and looks at his watch. Full moon outside over the murmuring night sea. The watch has stopped. He turns to Hugo: 'What time is it, Hugo?'

'It's only 8.30. Still too early to go to bed. Do you want me to take over the waiting?'

Hugo appears to possess some sort of mental timepiece and is never more than a few minutes wrong. He has something about watches or clocks, claims he will not be subject to the tyranny of time. It reminds Jake of his elder daughter who always hated to be photographed. Like primitive people, she said that cameras were ready to steal her soul.

The telephone rang.

That was unusual. Nobody had ever called them. Hugo grumbled in his sleep but didn't open his eyes. Jake picked the receiver up.

'Hello?'

'Hello, hello? I'm phoning about the job advertised in this week's paper. Is it still available? I can really type fast, you know.'

'Sorry to disappoint you, but you must have dialled a wrong number.'

'Really?'

'I'm afraid so. But we can keep on talking, if you don't mind; you have a lovely voice. Really sexy.'

'Sorry, I haven't really got the time. I have to find out about the job. I hope I didn't wake you up.'

'Not at all, I enjoyed talking to you. Bye.'

Later, Hugo asked him:

'Did she really have a pretty voice or were you just saying that to keep her hanging on?'

Jake laughed.

'No. This girl had a slightly husky voice, as if the words sort of came from her chest. Gave me the shivers.'

The sound of their voices echoed through the now virtually empty hotel as the night continued after the interruption. The resort town of Rainbow Alley slumbered on, waiting for the sunny season to return after the dull and uncommercial cycle of the inevitable year.

In the darker corner of the room, Hugo grinned like a Cheshire cat with a four-day growth of beard. Funny him asking that, thought Jake.

Funny hearing that characteristic husky voice again. He knew it was her, he could have sworn by it. Like electricity coursing through your body after sliding your wet tongue over a new, charged battery. Weird. He had spent madcap, crazy hours between the cotton sheets of the bed making love to her in all the most imaginative erotic positions, until the very joints of his body had moaned with pleasure. He had watched, entranced, as the tilting horizon of her pale buttocks had hovered in mid-air as her face slowly lowered itself down towards his genitals, her full breasts brushing against his stomach, her hair spread out over his chest and, later, after she had gone, he had found it so painfully difficult to remember her face.

Yes, the high cheekbones and dull complexion, the grey-blue-green eyes of ice, the unfortunate pimple lurking under her lower lip, yes he could catalogue all the individual details. The fading scar on her forehead where her hair began, the subtle change in colour of her nipples after the humid passage of his wandering tongue, but somehow all those memories would no longer fit together to form the total image of a face ...

Yet he was certain this was no feat of his imagination. He *had* known such a girl. She was as real as this Waiting Game in this anonymous hotel room in Rainbow Alley by the sea. Much too pretty to be untrue. Yeah. Was it his fault if he couldn't even recall her name?

Hugo was snoring.

Jake's attention on the dark landscape of sea and night wavered. He tried once more to remember, furrowing his brows.

They had just made love, her nails were still digging fiercely into the skin of his back, she had suddenly asked:

'Don't forget my name. Do to me anything that you want but, please, don't ever forget my name.'

Pain ran through him at the thought of that faraway night. He'd met her at a party. They had walked back to his flat holding hands, following the pattern of the river that ran through the city.

What was her name, what was her face like, the girl who'd also said 'I love you' in a possible moment of desperation, but he hadn't really wanted to hear and, conveniently, a heavy lorry had driven by outside the block, carrying a load of beetroots from Hamburg to the Galapagos Islands, so maybe he'd really heard her saying 'your feet are cold, love' or 'why are you always eating chocolate, love?'

She had left at two in the morning.

'Why don't you stay the night? It's cold outside.'

She had answered (this he remembered clearly):

'Haven't got the time. Really. There's a hovercraft leaving in the morning for Rainbow Alley. Someone there needs me more than you.'

In the now empty bed, he could still smell the fleeting odour of her absent body. She was dressing with hasty, slightly unco-ordinated movements. He had asked:

'Stay. Everybody knows that Rainbow Alley is at the bloody end of the world.'

Realising how little he knew of her.

How little he would remember.

Unknown to him, in the present, in a nearby room with strictly parallel geometry and matching furniture, Ingrid and the barman were sexually occupied, almost recreating these sad shards from his sentimental past.

A cloud moved over the darkened moon. Out there, the perimeter of the mirror of time shuddered violently as a sudden breeze wheezed out of nowhere in particular and animated the currents of the sky in a circular motion. Jake blinked. Could it be an optical illusion? Like a treacherous oasis in a desert when the senses are dulled by pain and urgent need? He looked again, squinting, trying to identify something out over the sea. Should he awaken Hugo? He looked once more, after rubbing his tired eyes. Odd shapes seemed to be moving behind the cloud, freeze-framed in the sky like evanescent, ghostly appearances. He rushed towards the bed to alert Hugo. By the time they had returned to the vantage point of the window, the abnormal cloud had faded and the moon had assumed its dominant position again. Everything appeared normal again.

Hugo looked at Jake, wonderingly.

A bell rang downstairs in the hotel lobby.

A new arrival.

Jake shuddered. Held Hugo's stare and said:

'Help. It feels just like being a prisoner in a fantasy story.'

'Just a coincidence,' Hugo reassured him as he moved back towards the warmth of the bed and the crumpled blankets.

In the morning, Jake woke up late. Hugo had gone down to breakfast already and snapped him out of slumberland on his return to the room. His first thought as the noise of the door slamming drew him up in fourth gear from a recurring dream of his life as a mosaic of women past, future and imagined was that he should phone home right away, talk to the children, assure them that it was nothing personal, that life was sometimes just too much, difficult to understand, that you one day just had to escape into another world, even if it was only temporary. As he drifted uncomprehendingly through layers of awareness a last vestige of dream saw him wondering whether his wife would be bra-less as she anxiously picked up the telephone. Hugo's voice shattered the unreality.

'It's a girl. She arrived during the night.'

'Oh,' muttered Jake.

'She's from somewhere in Scandinavia. Can't pronounce her name. Used to work as a travel clerk. Travelled through the night to get here. Great body.'

He didn't catch her name either, her accent was too thick and she spoke too fast.

'Back home, I was involved with a married man and our

relationship was going all wrong, you know. It wasn't my fault, really, but I have bad luck, things never work out the way they should. He was just too possessive. He was threatening to kill his wife in a fake car accident and run away with me. So I ran away first.'

Backstage at a rock and roll gig, the lead singer in a heavy metal group had made a pass at her. She'd felt flattered, there were much prettier groupies around in the dressing-room, but his performance in bed had been lazy and unenthusiastic. He was constantly high on one illegal substance or another and his post-coital conversation proved more interesting than his love-making. He had revealed to her how, two years ago back in a large South American town where the group had played the local football arena, he had been introduced to a beautiful aristocratic-looking socialite who had proved to be a witch. Jealous of the power that his music unwittingly gave him over large crowds, she had in a moment of folly stolen what she said was his magic. The very next day, she had died, shot through the right eye by a jealous American husband called McGuffin who had mistaken her for his wife; she had been wearing a similar Karl Lagerfeld dress which the adulterous woman also owned (although it was a copy). Ever since, the rock star had lost the charisma that drained multitudes to enormous sports arenas to attend his concerts, his records no longer hit the charts with bullets and his sales took a sharp downward spiral. Worse, he no longer enjoyed performing on stage, where once he had taunted the young girls with his writhing and calculated postures and tamed the mad rhythms of the air into a boogie dance beat with consummate ease and natural abandon.

As the blonde girl narrated her story, Jake tried to remember the features of Agnetha Eklander and was no longer certain whether this was her or not. The girl wore a floppy promotional sweat shirt stretched by too many washes and the shape of her body remained a secret.

She had followed the rock star, she continued, until the end of his farewell tour and had then joined him on a country farm where he intended to research the ancient lores in the hope of finding a way to recapture the old magic and banish his affliction to wherever it had come from. This is where, she explained, she had

first heard of the Newsky Prospekt games, particularly the
expedition to the other side of death. The rock star believed that
his magic, like Eurydice, was held entrapped on the other side,
the captive of some malevolent spell. As he progressed in his
research, he neglected her even more and she would spend most
of her days trying on decorous frocks from the star's unending
wardrobe, pretending to be another.

Then, one night, there had been a thunderous noise from the
musician's study. She had rushed down the stairs to investigate
the commotion and found he had disappeared, vanished into thin
air. The room was empty, just piles of books scattered all across,
open pages, broken spines. He was nowhere else to be found in
the house.

Hounded by investigative journalists after the mysterious dis-
appearance, the Scandinavian girl had fled and, following a
hunch and the memory of her all-too-rare conversations with the
musician, had hitch-hiked her way to Rainbow Alley to find the
façade of the hotel the only area emerging from the surrounding
darkness like a magnet.

'But how do we get there?' asked the barman who had listened
with rapt attention to the girl's tale, sighing sadly from time to
time as the story progressed. 'Your guitar-player guy found a
solution. Dying is mighty easy, but how do we know we'll really
reach the other side. We could just slit our throats and disappear
forever into a white light oblivion and bye bye baby bye bye.'

'I think I know a way,' said Hugo, smiling quietly in one
corner.

'But,' Jake protested mildly, 'we're not playing that game. Ours
is the waiting game. We can't change the rules halfway through.'

'Of course we can. Anyway, she's arrived, she's here, isn't she?'
his friend answered, pointing at the blonde girl with the high
cheekbones and the 'rock 'n' roll is here to stay' sweat shirt.

Jake reluctantly acquiesced.

'La petite mort – the little death,' Hugo said with a knowing
look at his now silent companions awaiting his words of wisdom
with bated breath. 'Besides,' as he later revealed to Jake, 'it's one
sure way of getting to sleep with her. She intrigues me. I just
know she'll be perfect in the sack. Certainly gives one something
to look forward to, doesn't it?'

Jake gulped at Hugo's brazen cheek. For one second or two, it was all he could do not to hit him squarely in the jaw with his clenched fist. But Hugo kept on smiling in that ingenuously disarming way he had. Obviously, he couldn't quite see what Jake would find so preposterous about the whole thing.

Jake recovered quickly and said to Hugo: 'It's a bit much. I like her too, you know.'

'Yes, but you're too much of a romantic. You'd like to be an experienced sensualist, but in your heart, where it matters, you're just a softie!'

'I don't agree. Not one bit.'

'You wouldn't, would you?'

When Jake finally resolved to phone home, his wife did pick up the receiver but slammed it back down again as soon as she recognised his voice.

'Bloody hell!'

He helped himself to a soft drink from the bar. The others were in one of the upstairs rooms with two double beds up to he knew not what in sexual experiments. He thought of the dream Agnetha Eklander and also of the blonde Scandinavian travel clerk upstairs enjoying the caresses of Hugo and the barman and, maybe also, plump little Ingrid and blushing wildly as the excesses accumulated and her senses came alive as fingers, lips, bodies and extremities flared in an extra dimension of lust and desire. He was jealous. He couldn't stand the thought of others exploring her intimacy, guiding her movements, touching her where . . .

He closed his eyes. He felt like crying or shouting out loud that it wasn't fair, that *he* wanted to take her down to the beckoning beach and make love to her, with no others around to mock his acute sensitivity, his feelings.

He stood up.

Hesitated a short instant.

Then rushed towards the lift. Pressed the call button which shone red. A few minutes passed. He thought he could imagine their laughter percolating all the way down the lift shaft as he waited. No, couldn't be them. He was just torturing himself. Still no lift. He moved to the stairs and began climbing them two or three steps at a time. A moment later he was finally at the top, out of breath, his body aching all over from lack of fitness.

He made his way down the dimly lit hotel corridor, breathing hard, trying to control the frenzy of anguish racing through his heart. The door was open.

The room was empty, as he had half-expected it to be somehow. The furniture was in topsy-turvy disarray, the sheets on both beds crumpled and stained. Like a landscape after the battle. They were gone. Hugo's crazy scheme had succeeded somehow. Only he was left behind.

This time, Jake allowed the tears to flow, out of both sorrow and self-pity.

Winter moved on.

With the approaches of spring, a few tourists began making occasional timid forays onto the beach. One morning, Jake walked down to the shore and followed the line of the coast until the silhouette of Rainbow Alley's roofs and hotels dimmed in the distance behind him. There was a big circular rock standing like a fallen object from outer space right in the middle of the sand, sheltered from the inland by a steep grey cliff. Jake somehow managed to climb to the top of the rock, breaking most of his nails and scraping the top skin off his left knee in the process.

Once there, he looked out towards the sea, peered at the now neglected mirror of time and muttered to himself:

'If only I could fly like a bird, then I'd escape through the mirror.'

And night came again, following the natural laws of the physical world, as Jake shivered, waiting on his rock for his wings to grow.

Back in the land of death, Agnetha Eklander walked along with bare breasts.

Robert Holdstock's novella *Mythago Wood* won the award for the best British SF and fantasy story of the year and will soon be part of a long-awaited novel of the same title. A young author who lives in Hertfordshire, Holdstock is an ex-zoologist with several critically-acclaimed novels to his credit: *Necromancer, Earthwind, Where Time Winds Blow*, etc...

The Boy who Jumped the Rapids

Robert Holdstock

The horn-helmeted man had come from the far west, following the ridgeways and woodland tracks, and crossing streams and rivers at the nearest point, not at their shallows. From the state of his clothes it was clear that he had journeyed through the dark forests where the Belgic peoples ruled; from the downwind smell of him, the hint of salt and sea, it was clear that he had travelled across the wide ocean that separated two lands. His hair hung lank and fire-red from beneath his strange helmet, a helmet with stubby horns and sparkling decorations. When the sun was bright the helmet flashed in the way of gold, and sometimes in the way of silver. And again, sometimes it gleamed in the way of bronze. But there was no iron there, not that the boy Caylen could see.

Word had already gone ahead to the forest community of Caswallon's people, and now only Caylen and two men discreetly trailed the stranger as he ran along the high ground, squinting at times into the distance, seeking smoke, perhaps, or the sea. Caylen moved stealthily through the undergrowth, pausing occasionally to watch the horned man as he ran and danced past in the open. The boy had never seen anything, or anyone, quite like this dark-cloaked foreigner; he didn't walk like a warrior; nor did he run, crouched and wary, like a hunter. He ran upright, his cloak streaming behind him, a narrow, skin-wrapped object held firmly in his right hand. At times he actually leapt into the air, twisting about and spinning as he touched the ground again so that his cloak swirled about him. His voice, at these times, was a loud cry, a triumphant cry, echoing away across the woodlands, and the grassy downs, and frightening the dark carrion birds that nested in the spruce and ash trees.

At dusk the man came down from the ridgeway and followed

the tracks, of hunters and animals both, through the forest until
he came to the tall, wooden totem that stood where the river
forked. This was the holy place at the apex of the streams.

Within minutes he had found the village, though the village
had been expecting him from before noon.

He stood outside the heavy palisade, outside the open gate,
and stared across the muddy compound at the low round-
houses, the broken animal pens, the roped dogs, hysterical in
their excitement and barking loudly, the huddle of women in
their drab green robes, the children, excitedly gathered in a
goat-house, peering at the stranger through the thin, wicker
walls. He looked also at the line of dark-haired men who stood
facing him, their spears and swords held across their chests.
Chickens, ducks and grey puppies ran noisily between them,
disturbed in their empty-headed ways by the tension in the air.

The man said one word, which might have been 'Food'. He
said it loudly, and there was something in his voice that made
the pain of his empty belly obvious. Then he said, 'Help', or a
word that sounded similar. His eyes glazed a moment as he
looked around at the people of the village, and then he flung
back his cloak and held the long, thin package above his head.
'Help,' he repeated, and lowered the object to his lips, hugging
it afterwards as he might hug a child. 'Rianna,' he said, but the
name was strange to Caswallon and his kin, and they ignored it.

When at last the Chieftain, Caswallon – who was Caylen's
father – stepped towards the horned man, it was to welcome
him. The man removed his gleaming helmet and stepped inside
the palisade. His scalp, below the helm, had been scarred
savagely by a sword. Caylen grimaced at the sight of the
hideous wound, and the thought of the agony this man must
have borne.

It rained as it always rained in the forest: hard, for a while,
driving man and beast into shelter; then gentle, almost like a
sea spray. The rolling storm clouds passed away into the east,
and the sky brightened. The children were driven out into the
gleaming mud pond that had formed within the village walls,
and set about the task of laying straw and wood walkways.
When they had finished, they gathered the animals from the

edge of the woodlands, chased them back into the compound, and then sneaked away among the trees.

Caylen followed the boys at a distance. The day before, he had suffered a beating from the two sons of his father's cousin, the warrior Eglin, blinded during a raid three years ago. These two boys were vicious and compassionless. They joked about their father in an open and openly derisory way, calling him 'blind stick', and bragging that they would have taken his head a long time before but it would not have been worth the effort. They spared no wrath from Caylen, stripping him and bruising him with malicious glee. They had carved something on his backside, but the scarring and scratching had obscured its nature from his friend, Fergus, who had helped Caylen to his special place, near the river, and bathed and patched the wound.

'Don't tell my father,' Caylen had said, and Fergus had laughed.

'What would *he* do? Nothing! He'd do nothing. Not even with the stranger here.'

Caylen had laughed angrily and said he knew that, but he always hoped that one day Caswallon would step in and defend his son from the other village children. It was a vain hope.

Now, with Fergus, he followed the pack, keeping low in the undergrowth that lined a narrow boar-run. The other children walked boldly along the trampled bracken, snagging clothes on bramble and thorn and noisily knocking aside the wood and plant growth with sword sticks.

'That ol' pig'll hear them,' said Fergus. 'But it won't attack. Not until it thinks it's safe, and that will be us. So let's hurry.'

Caylen needed no second urging. He raced along the run and only dropped to a crouch when he saw the bobbing heads of the other boys, in front of him, and of course on that heart-stopping occasion when he realised he was standing right by the thicket where the boar was calmly waiting for the noise to pass. He could smell it in there, musty, fetid; its breathing was rapid, almost hoarse. He thought he saw a shaft of sun glint off the cruel, curved tusks, and he realised this was a giant boar, a huge thing, that had probably come down from the deep forests inland.

Caswallon knew it was here, but it was taboo to kill boars for two seasons, because of the goring of the druid Glamach, in the season of Bel. It would make great eating, this one, and was a severe threat to the village while it was alive. But until the season of the fires, and the blessing of Lug, it would forage the near-woods unhindered.

Caylen leapt past it and waited for Fergus. Fergus was a small lad, two years younger than the wiry Chieftain's son, and his face was red with effort, his tawny hair slick and plastered with animal grease which ran down his cheeks as the heat in his flesh melted it. He clutched a tiny wooden knife, and there was such an expression of childish excitement in his face that Caylen felt his own excitement surge again. They went on, breaking through the tangled, thorny undergrowth where the ground was marshy, and finding a clearer passage through the gnarled trunks of oak and elm, where bluebells covered the ground in a single, dazzling azure sheen. The other boys had gone through here too, and Fergus led the way after them, diving from tree to tree, listening to the rustling in the distance, and the sound of bird life disturbed by the intruders below.

When they were near the clearing known as Old Stone Hollow, Caylen led the way to the side. They wormed through nettles, hands behind their necks, and found an old trickle-stream, dried now that summer had been halfway exhausted. From this they peered, through dried bracken and the tangle of a rose bush, at the small, grassy clearing, with the great wind and rain-etched boulder poking up from deep in the ground. In front of this rock a small, wooden shelter had been built, and the red-haired man, stripped to the waist, was busy hammering iron nails into the sloping roof. No house, then, but a shrine of some sort. Smoke rose from his tiny fire, and a fish slowly grilled there. The wrapped object that was so precious to him stood against the boulder. Caylen could see that the man had painted things on that stone, strange shapes and symbols, and pictures of animals too. They were painted in blue and green, and he had painted similar symbols on his arms, and on his chest. Caylen knew of the tribes in the north and east who painted their bodies in this way, but this one was from the west, from the far west, or so his father had said in Caylen's hearing, from the land across a great sea, where a thousand Kings ruled.

He didn't even speak their language, although he had learned enough words to indicate his needs. He was here because he was a fugitive, because he was protecting something from evil forces in his homelands.

After a while Caylen grew restless. He drew back from the glade, Fergus following, and began to walk towards the river. They were puzzled by the man, and intrigued, and they were aware, too, that Caswallon and the other villagers were uneasy with him, although he was in no way hostile.

Abruptly they were surrounded by boys, and Caylen felt a stinging blow on his face where a spiky, green nut had been thrown. There was laughter, and the screech of boyish anger that precedes a boyish punishment. But Caylen was in no mood for trouble and he found his temper at exactly the right moment, swinging a dead stick with a loud whack against the leader's head.

He was off then, the boys in pursuit. Where Fergus went he didn't know, and for the moment didn't care. His backside still hurt, and the head that he had struck had belonged to the boy whose knife had carved the pain. They chased him, shouting and yelling, but he was surefooted and swift, and knew the way to the river better than they. He ducked through dense stands of oak, and plunged into bramble thickets, not caring about the scratches to his legs and arms, preferring that pain to the pain of the senseless beatings.

The boys closed on him where the forest thinned, but now he could hear the water, the rushing waters of the great river, and he sensed he was safe, even though a part of his mind still questioned the strangeness of the fact.

He ran down the bank, waded in and felt the river's coldness sting all the way to his waist. The flow was gentle, the mud below soft and sucking. It was a long way across, a good minute's wade, and then he scrambled out, just as Domnorix led the gang of panting youths out of the woods and to the water's edge. Fergus appeared, farther away, and shook his head, smiling but smiling uncertainly. He crouched, exactly as Caylen was crouching, and stared at the gentle water.

The boys threw stones for a while, which Caylen dodged with arrogant ease, even lobbing a few back. Domnorix taunted him. 'Only a demon could get across those rapids. Only someone possessed by evil magic could float across those waters. You're an evil thing, Caylen, your father knows it, your mother knows it. Evil. Evil.' And others cried, 'Possessed, possessed!' And still others taunted him with, 'Unbirthed, unbirthed!' or, 'Crow's spawn, crow's spawn!'

All of this Caylen had heard a hundred times before, and so he sat on the river bank and grinned, watching the boys across the calm waters until they went away.

Fergus walked down to stand across from him. 'How *do* you get across, Caylen?' he called, and smiled almost nervously, as if he didn't want to hear the answer.

'I've told you,' said Caylen, not angrily, but with a patience that he was determined to preserve for this one friend of his. 'I waded across. The water is *calm*. Why don't you try it? It's easy.'

Fergus shook his head. He looked at the river, then at Caylen, and he seemed lost; he was more of a child than his nine years made him; and he needed Caylen very much. He seemed stick thin in his baggy cotton trousers and ragged shirt, his limbs scratched by bramble and thorn. Across the water the two boys watched each other, each longing for closer company, each aware that they were united in friendship through the vagaries of life in such a small community.

'No one could wade through that, Caylen,' Fergus said. 'You have a trick, don't you? There's a way across that we can't see, but which you found. Tell me where it is ... go on, tell me!'

'It's right in front of you,' urged Caylen, and now a sudden edge of desperation entered his voice, and his manner. He stood up, tossed a pebble into the river. It splashed and the water was so calm that the ripple was able to spread slowly outwards before it was carried away. Above the placid surface, Caylen could glimpse the ghostly image of the tumbling rapids; faintly, he could hear their rush. 'Please, Fergus ... Please! Wade across. Honestly, there's nothing dangerous here, nothing at all.'

Fergus shivered, wrapped his arms about his shoulders and again shook his head. His eyes were kindly, his smile telling Caylen that it was all right, that though he didn't dare wade across, it wasn't going to change their friendship.

Oh Fergus, thought Caylen desperately. If you would just find the courage not to believe your eyes, to come across to me. That would show the other boys that I'm not some evil spirit. It would convince my father that the things I see are not abnormal, not unnatural. One friend, bearing out my word, and it could be so different, and the chief of the village would not have to stay hidden in the forests for the shame of his son.

But Fergus had heard movement in the woods and waved a brief farewell to Caylen before slipping into the gloom of the undergrowth. Caylen saw a figure passing along the river, hidden by darkness and the bramble thickets. For a second he saw the gleam of sun on metal, and made out the stubby horns of the stranger's helmet. But then that glimpse had been lost in the great confusion of movement as a brisk wind disturbed everything, including the river. Caylen sat for a long while watching for the horned man, but he had gone.

The wind dropped, and with its passing Caylen realised what an unnatural wind it had been, neither a summer breeze, nor a storm wind blowing in advance of a fall of torrential rain. It had been wind like a breath, blowing in a wide circle so that the branches of trees moved one way, and across the river blew oppositely; it was a warm wind, like the passing of some spirit, and Caylen felt the hair on his neck prick up with apprehension. He looked up the river, and down, but saw nothing apart from the wide, gentle waters as they curved from north to south.

Behind him the forest was eerily still. Small animal trackways led through it to the rising hills deeper inland, and the overgrown valleys of a country into which none of the people of Caswallon had ever ventured. From the tree tops on the village side of the river those hills could be seen, cloud-shadowed, green, and the marks of a ridgeway were obvious. But it was a ridgeway that no man had ever travelled, or could remember anyone having ever travelled. There were those who had sought it; it would have made easier passage of the journey north to the edge of the truly deep and dense forests where no tribes lived and the hunting was good. But however the voyager approached that ridge he came upon some impossible barrier – the rapids, or cliffs, or impenetrable, marshy woodlands. The land beyond the rapids was a mystery, even to the boy who could see beyond the illusion of danger.

Caylen had ventured through the silent tangle-woods only once, and that was recently. He had stood in a clearing by a wood-choked stream, and looked up the slopes of a hill. He had thought he could hear the sound of a village on the other side. But as he had tried to cross the blocked stream he had become suddenly overwhelmed with fear, and had turned and run frantically back to the river.

Strangely, he had known that the fear was mere foolishness, more of the illusion that guarded this piece of land from the rest of his village.

Still, he felt something of that apprehension now as he stood and faced the gloomy woodland. He took a deep breath, lobbed a stone among the trees, then took a few paces towards them, kicking through the fern and bracken until he was fully shaded by the foliage.

As his eyes grew accustomed to the gloom he could see the metal totem standing there. Tall, spindly legged, its arms reaching outwards, its eyes wide and dead . . . He caught just a glimpse of it as sun broke through the foliage, and he could see that it was silvery, metallic, like some iron god erected at the edge of a tribal land. There was a sound, a wailing like some banshee, but it was distant and it merely made him glance about, frightened.

He walked a little deeper into the forest, picking his way carefully. The place was unnaturally silent, no birds, no rustling of wind-blown foliage. He felt he was being watched.

At the wood-clogged stream, again the heart-stopping fear snagged at him, but he fought it down, stepped over the rotting carcasses of tree and branch, and came, within a few paces, to a thistle-choked clearing.

What he saw here astonished him. It was the ruin of a building made all of stone. It rose nearly as high as an oak, and its windows were straight sided, perfectly regular. Creepers, ivy, weeds of all sorts had grown up through the strange structure, adding to its aura of desertion.

Caylen had heard of stone buildings – in the north of his own lands, it was said, houses were made of white stones piled one on another; and across the ocean, in lands where the sun shone all year round, there was a race of warlike men who built stone houses as high as the clouds.

A thin strip of iron surrounded the ruined building. It hummed softly and when Caylen reached to touch it he felt an unpleasant tingling on his skin that made him draw back.

The next moment a bat shrieked down close to him, its audible screech so loud in his ear that he himself screamed, and turned and ran, watching as the huge night-beast circled twice through the trees, its wings outstretched, its mouth still emitting that supernatural cry. It was gone, then, into the woods, back to its daytime resting place.

Caylen caught his breath, tried to stop his hands trembling, then walked shakily back to the river and quickly crossed it.

He stood on the far bank for a moment, and stared at the water. He could see the great swirling rapids. Jagged rocks poked up and broke that awesome flow of water, as they would break a man who slipped and was carried onto them. He watched the raging foam-covered river, and the drowning eddies, and he looked through them at the placid river as it truly was. He would never understand why only he could see beyond this illusion, and he would never understand who created the dream, and why.

But for the moment he was cold, and wet. His heart was still racing, and his body was still tied in knots of fear, the sort of fear that not even a rampaging wild boar would normally induce in him.

Every day the horned man came to the village for food and drink, and every day he sat and for a while tried to communicate with Caswallon and the others. The sense of unease was almost tangible. Not a man crouched without his sword, even the stranger, who detected the tension and was wary of a sudden fury. To thank the village for their help he spent a whole day rebuilding a ruined outhouse, a thatched building, more than a man's height from the ground to point, roomy enough inside for the sheep to huddle when the winter snows covered the forest and made the ground hard as rock.

The job was finished swiftly; the stranger was skilled at his job, and of course, once he had tokened his gratitude by working alone for an hour, the others helped. He placed his helmet on his head, then, and towards dusk ran back into the forest, his black cloak flowing behind him. When Caylen ventured near to his glade, even though it was night, he could hear the sound of building, the expansion of the ceremonial place that the stranger was constructing for his own ends.

After a week the sounds of hammering could no longer be heard, and the stranger had vanished. None ventured to the glade itself, for Caswallon had warned that until the horned man communicated otherwise the glade was his, since he had requested it.

That which he built there was a temple, a shrine, a tomb . . . that which he buried there was more precious to him than life itself. Not a man, nor a woman, nor child from the village was allowed to interfere with this burial, until the stranger departed and took his memories with him, leaving only the monument in Old Stone Hollow, which would pass under the care of the village.

After a week of nights made restless by rain and Caswallon's continuing despair with his son, Caylen, word came of warriors approaching along the ridgeway from the west. Red-haired, black-cloaked, they came fast, and with weapons. They sought the horn-helmeted man, and they were coming to kill him.

Caylen was crouched in the corner of his father's house as this news was brought. He had a fever, and his throat was sore. He was miserable because the druid had recommended that he be starved for a week, to help the illness, and to give a chance for those who had sent his evil to take him away. 'The body, unresisting, can be taken by the dark world,' he had told Caylen's father, and then had come and smeared foul-smelling substances on his lips and eyes and ears, and cut off a lock of his greased hair. This he had tied to a rabbit bone and slowly burned on the fire. Caswallon had watched all this, crouched close to the warmth, his strong features sad in the firelight, his eyes filled with anger, and remorse, and not even a hint of pity for his son.

'Is there no way to shake the possession? To make him like us, a man among men?'

The druid, squatting and eating his father's food as he burned the hair, shook his head. He was not an old man, but his lank grey hair, and untrimmed beard, gave him a wild look, and an aged appearance. His woollen tunic was dyed blue and cut short to the knees. He wore animal-bone beads and sparkling torques of bronze on each upper arm and round his neck. He was painted with mud, of course, the grey mud from the far-off rivers close to the sea. The mud on his body was to protect him from the evil presence in Caylen, that which made the boy able to jump over water and walk through the sheer cliff wall known as Wolfback.

'It's just a hill,' Caylen had said (two years before). 'A gentle hill, with boulders. There's no cliff!' He had walked among the stumpy trees and jutting stones, making his way up the rise of the slope. The men of the village had hung back, horrified. When Caylen walked further, there was a sudden panic. The druid, Glamach, had screamed a torrent of abuse at him, and made passes with his hands that effectively condemned Caylen to the dark fires.

Afterwards, when the shock had gone, and only the resentment remained, Caylen had sought out his friend Fergus. Fergus was terrified, then puzzled, and finally cried against his friend and confessed his confusion.

'But what did it *look* like I did?' Caylen asked.

'Can't you see them?' Fergus begged, pointing to the hill. There was a sheer cliff there, Fergus explained, and at the base of the cliff were sharpened spikes of wood on which were impaled the bloody corpses of men and women, and below the corpses, the bones of others. The air was strong with the stink of decaying flesh. Whoever lived beyond the cliff was dangerous. But Caylen had walked through the spikes and the corpses, and then right on up to the cliff itself, passing through the rock as if it had not been there.

Caylen looked hard, narrowing his eyes. When cloud shadowed the sun he imagined he could glimpse the spikes; but it was like a dream, a ghostly image that didn't last.

'He must be killed,' the druid was saying, in Caswallon's lodge. Hostile eyes, high-lit by the red fire, watched Caylen from across the room. 'But killed in the correct way. As yet I have not decided how best to use the spilling of his blood for the good of the village, and the cleansing of the stain of possession that is on it.'

And as if the words had induced in Caswallon a warlike anger, the man came across the lodge and stared down at his son, then raised his hand and dealt him such a blow that Caylen cried out. The cry fuelled the fires of hatred and frustration and Caswallon struck him again and again, dizzying him with the constant blows to the head. When the fury was passed, Caylen slumped back in his corner and sobbed. The druid came across to him and bathed his face in a pungent liquid, murmuring the secret words as he went, and calming the boy.

The pain passed away, but not the hurt. Caylen decided that he must leave the village and flee to his own special land, the land across the water where none of the village dared go. He rose after dusk, when the sky was twilight, and the forest quiet and dark. He ran lightly through the compound and entered the woods. But he had been seen and the slight, fleet-footed shape of Fergus came after him. 'I heard the beating,' he said. 'What are you going to do?'

'Go across the water and live there. It's the only safe place. The druid says I must be killed in a special way.'

Fergus grimaced. 'Horrible, horrible. I've seen a special killing. It's horrible.'

'I don't need you to tell me that,' said Caylen grimly. But he was glad of Fergus' company. It made his life bearable, if not attractive.

'I'll come with you across the rapids,' said Fergus, and in the twilight Caylen saw that his friend was crying.

'I'm glad,' he said. 'You'll be quite safe. And when we're old enough we'll raid the village and take all the women. That'll teach them.'

'Good idea,' said Fergus, wiping a hand across his eyes. Caylen could see that he was genuinely frightened; having made the declaration to cross the river he could not now back down. He was sad for his friend, so brutally treated by the village, and now he was frightened by his own rashness.

Someone stirred in the lodge, and it would not be long before Caswallon noticed that his demon son had slipped away. Before tonight this would not have bothered Caswallon; but Caylen suspected that from now until they killed him they would not allow him to leave the village. It was now or never, his last chance for freedom and peace.

They ran along the boar track, passing the thicket with hardly a glance, though they could hear the animal in there, snuffling sleepily. Without thinking they burst into Old Stone Hollow, where the small wooden temple had been built. Caylen stopped, catching his breath in surprise. His intention had been to go to the river, and unthinkingly he had come here. Fergus had just followed blindly, not really wanting to leave his friend, not wanting to think too hard about what was happening.

It was quite dark, but the moon, a fairly full crescent shining through the thin, wind-blown clouds, gave light enough to show what the stranger had made of his shrine. He had built it high, and wide, and he had built it all about the stone in the centre of the glade. A wide open doorway led to the interior. Inside, on the floor, Caylen could see a small tallow candle burning, its yellow flame hardly enough to show him anything of the interior. The wood of the shrine was fresh hewn, and expertly chopped into thick and lasting planks; it was bright, not yet dulled either by pitch or rain. Nor, yet, was it carved, though it would surely be represented with the symbols of the gods before the stranger was finished.

Caylen, feeling now that he had little to lose by any action, boldly stepped up to the shrine, and with Fergus following nervously behind, ducked and stepped inside.

The stone rose from the ground; the floor was still rough grass and the remnants of thorn and nettle. It smelled rich and earthy inside, though near to the door there was the pleasant tang of fresh cut wood, and near to the stone the musty smell of a tomb, the rock and all the grey dust that clung to it exuding an odour that was unmistakable.

On the stone rested a spear, and Caylen picked up the candle so he could see it better. This, he was quite sure, was what had been in the protective hides. A spear, a precious weapon, which the horn-helmeted man had carried from his land of kings, hiding it from his pursuers, rescuing it, no doubt, from those who would abuse whatever power it contained.

Unhesitatingly, Caylen picked it up and hefted it; nearly a man's height in length, it was carved from some dark wood, but lightweight, and the shaft was inscribed with rings and patterns from the very tip of it, to where the wide, leaf-shaped blade was fastened to the wood. The blade was iron, grooved and serrated, and on each side of the central rib there had been scratched an eye. It was the spear not of a warrior, for no warrior's spear could be so small, but of a child, a child's weapon, as deadly as any flung on the field of battle; the spear of a prince.

A hand reached past Caylen and took the weapon from him. He started with shock, gasped and turned to find himself looking up at the heavy features of the stranger, who stood with Fergus gripped firmly in his other hand, the palm stifling any sound his friend would have made.

Caylen tried to run, but the man used the spear to block his path. Then he let go of Fergus and smiled at them both, raised finger to lip and gently placed the spear back on the stone. He dropped to a crouch, now looking up at Caylen, who was a tall lad. His wild eyes were bright in the candle flame, his teeth gleaming white, his breath sweet as if he had been eating berries. His hands on their arms were strong, gentle. He looked from one to the other, but mostly he looked at Caylen. 'Come,' he said. 'Tell. Come, tell,' and as he spoke he rose, picked up the spear, and led the way from the shrine. Caylen hesitated only a second before following, and Fergus (with one compulsive grip of Caylen's hand, the squeeze of reassurance from one who is mortally afraid) also went after the stranger, out into the moonlit night, and into the forest.

They walked at first, Caylen keeping pace well along the overgrown animal trackways and through the bramble thickets. Fergus straggled a little, but every time they passed through a clearing in the forest he raced after Caylen and caught up, tugging once on Caylen's shirt to let him know that he was there again. The horned man, his helmet gleaming in the moonlight, paced on, and Caylen sensed he walked faster and faster, his cloak billowing behind him, catching on branches and rose thorns, but always tearing free. Suddenly the man made a sound, like a bird cry, but deep and long. He raised his arms, still walking, and then said a single word, 'Follow,' before he began to run.

Caylen ran too, and Fergus after, and they both watched as the horned man leapt high, then crouched low, twisting and turning as he ran until he became a source of crashing, stumbling, shrieking darkness, his helmet, the metal of his belt and necklet, flashing and glinting in the stray silvery light. His cloak swirled about his body, at times a wing, at other times a flowing robe of darkness, and always he ran, the forest loud with the sound of his noisy progress, and with the laughing and shrieking of the boys who followed.

Caylen joined the spirit of the wild dance, leaping and twisting himself, and staggering as he landed, struggling to keep his balance. He struck branches and tree trunks, and waved his hands through bracken and fern, and through the tight clumps of flower-covered moss; he felt everything in the forest, letting its night dew soak his clothes and his skin. The horned man jumped higher, touching branches more than twice his height above the ground, and at times, as he ran, Caylen thought he was actually walking through the air. He seemed to leap into the forest sky, and run through the very foliage, before gently landing and spinning round, his arms outstretched, his body whirling in the gloom.

At length, breathless, they came to the river, and Caylen realised that this was the illusory river that guarded his private haven. The man had led their merry dance in a wide and perfect circle. They were nearly back to the glade, but here he stopped, and reached to brush water across his perspiring face.

Caylen could almost hear the rushing of the waters, but the sound was on the edge of a waking dream, a distant sound, unreal, unrealised. He looked at Fergus and Fergus smiled brightly, not speaking the words but almost saying that he would still wade across with Caylen the next time Caylen went.

The stranger had torn a strip of bark from a tree and now he pushed his dagger twice through the wood and made two holes for eyes. This woody mask he held against his face, peering at the boys through the slits. He spoke to them, then, in their own tongue, in perfect language, his voice thrilling them with its texture of sound, soft yet deep, a woodland sound, a wild sound. While he was speaking he kept the mask of bark to obscure his lips from them.

'Like you, she was young, full of the wonder of life. A girl of looks so fair that she caught every heart, was sought by every king in our king-ridden lands. Her name was Rianna. She was not the daughter of a king, but she was a princess, and it was a king who guarded her when his own soldiers razed her village and killed her kinfolk. A compassionate king, who looked at her, the tender child, and never again raised his army against the land. He built a great stone fort, a great city, and shaped a great people. Rianna was the queen of that people, not in rank, but in heart. No man or

woman could tear their gaze away from young Rianna. She was a
child born to be a queen, a queen born to be a goddess.

'But the great land, and the great king, fell to a dark host from
the north, men without feeling, men of war. They swept through
the hills and took the stone fort, putting to the sword all who were
noble born. They chased families into the hills and marshes,
subjugated every town that had known this time of peace. This is
the way in our land, and it was the king who was wrong, to be
unprepared and unwilling for battle. And yet, none of his people
condemned him, even though he had betrayed them. One thing
kept hope alive. Rianna. Rianna had escaped the butchery, and
the conquest, for on the eve of the invasion a man had come out of
the night, out of the earth itself, and taken this girl from the fort.
He fled with her to safety. She took only her clothes and her
childish spear, the weapon fashioned to mark her adoption to the
royal line.

'This is how it ended for her: in a valley, mist-obscured and
deep, where not even animals ventured for fear of the emptiness
of the place, there went Rianna, carried by the man of earth, that
clay man who had come from the grave to take her beyond the
savagery of the northern host. But another went there, one of that
dark host who knew too well the danger of the girl should she
return a queen and draw the people to her. He found her, and
before her guardian could act he turned her own spear against
her, twisted the blade in her heart to ensure the deed was properly
done. But the earth one, before she died, had magicked her spirit
to the very blade of the spear. Here she lives, and while she lives
so the people of her land live in hope. Here is that spear. Here is
Rianna. I have brought her to these lands, for safety, to erect a
shrine to her, to protect her for the years while the storm passes in
our country.'

The horn-helmeted man ceased to speak, and he moved the
mask from his face. Caylen saw the tears there, and watched in
silence as he raised the blade of the spear to his lips and kissed it,
kissed the iron that had once tasted so bitter with the blood of his
young queen. He looked towards the river, then raised the mask
again. 'This place I saw in a dream. There are other places like it,
concealed, guarded. Powerful places. But this is the one that was
shown to me.'

Caylen watched him, curiously disturbed. In the same way that when he stared at the rapids he saw only the calm waters that were the truth of the river, so, as the man had spoken, the flowery, sad words of the story had fallen away. Caylen had been aware of the flowing, rather pleasant tongue that was the stranger's natural language; he had been aware, too, of starker, less romantic images: a cold, bleak stone fort, a desolate, windswept land, a bloody battle, a complacent warlord, gruesome slaughter, an escape into the night for a screaming, terrified girl, a mercenary sent to kill her, and achieving that end swiftly and brutally.

Time had passed more swiftly than the reason could accommodate, and Caylen was startled as he heard the first chorus of forest birds, marking their awareness of the dawn. Turning, where he sat, he saw the glow of light in the east, above the trees, above the water. Fergus was sleeping, and Caylen grinned as he saw this. The horned man seemed to smile as well, and Caylen turned to him.

'Then you claim to be a magician, a man with dark powers, who uses them for good purpose ...'

The stranger inclined his head. From behind the mask he said, 'Dark powers? Not I. None save the power to run without stopping.'

'But why did you come to save her, why ride from the earth? Who were you that you felt the need to save her, to bring her to safety?'

The horn-helmeted man laughed, but the laugh was bitter, not amused. 'You have misunderstood me, young Caylen. I was the man who followed them. I was the man who killed her.'

Five men came, like braying hounds, down from the ridgeway and through the glades of the forest until they found the village, following the spoor of the man they pursued. They talked for an hour with Caswallon, but the village was weak in arm when compared to such seasoned soldiers as these. Caswallon spoke firmly with one of the strangers who had a smattering of the village tongue; at no time did he bend to any whim of theirs, but from the outset it was clear that he would not hinder them in their quest. Each of these men was sturdily built, and heavily bearded; long hair, bound back with green linen, was ungreased and fair;

they carried round shields on their back, made of alder and beaten leather, rimmed and studded with iron; they carried fighting spears and throwing darts, and each wore a sword so richly decked and turned with gold and silver on the pommel that there could be no question of their nobility, and their warrior status.

Caylen saw them as he walked, unsuspecting, from the woods. Even as he turned to run back to the Old Stone Hollow, and the shrine of Rianna, so Caswallon was pointing the way to the glade, and the chase was on.

The guardian of the shrine heard Caylen coming towards him, through the thickets, along the old boar trail. The boar had gone two nights previous, foraging in some other part of the forest, perhaps tired of the activity in its vicinity. When Caylen burst from the trees, breathless, screaming, the man already had the spear, and was fleeing towards the river.

The horned man stumbled, and Caylen caught up with him. As he helped the man to his feet the sound of the pursuers was loud, close; they seemed to know every twist, every turn that their prey had taken. They had followed him across two lands and an ocean, and they had not put a step wrong.

The man staggered to his feet, but his leg was twisted. Wild-eyed, fearful for more than his own life, he thrust the spear at Caylen, pressed it on him, and said to him to run swiftly and cross the illusory river. 'It will be safe there, safe with you. Guard her, Caylen. Guard little Rianna, as I have guarded her since I took her life.'

Caylen turned and fled, the man staggering after him, but slow, now, and crying with the pain.

Caylen found the river. Clutching the spear he ran through the shallows, emerging cold and wet on the other side. He could hear the sound of children, approaching along the far bank, but all he could see for the moment was his friend Fergus, racing towards him, tears in his eyes.

Then the horned man came through the trees, cried loud and fell to his knees, his face racked with pain, yet smiling. For a moment he stared at Caylen, met the boy's gaze and raised his arm towards him. Rianna, he cried, and again, and again, until a fair-haired man stepped up behind him and dealt him a blow with his sword that cut through the bone and sinew of his neck. The sound of Rianna's name died on his lips, spilled to the wind as his dark blood spilled to the earth.

Caylen ran away from the river, towards the woods, and felt the prickle of fear, fear of the unknown, fear of the magic force that worked here to keep this place of hill and woodland guarded from mortal man. He squatted then, the spear held across his lap, his hand resting lightly on the vibrant, cold metal blade. The hunters prowled up and down the water's edge, but none ventured to try and cross; all were taken by that vital fear, induced not just by the violent waters, but by the wall of magic that was dazzling their senses.

They called to him in their strange, flowing tongue, and sometimes they were begging him, and sometimes they were threatening him. Domnorix and four of the village boys were crouched some yards away, afraid to come closer to the strangers. Only Fergus stood with them, watching Caylen through wide, fear-filled eyes.

Caylen clutched the spear tighter. He was safe here, and so was the memory of Rianna, and he would never go home, never in all his life. He would stay here and hide her, and he knew that when the time was right some man of earth would come for her, to take her home.

But how could he have forgotten Fergus? Fergus, who had been his friend through the weeks of hatred and the months of pain; the young boy who had counted his friendship with Caylen so high that he had determined to break through his fear of magic, and follow Caylen across the river. 'Wait for me!' he cried, and Caylen came to his feet in shock, and with a great cry of, 'No, go back! No, Fergus, not now, not now!' he raced to the water's edge, the spear gripped tightly in his right hand.

'I'm coming with you,' shouted Fergus, confusion painting panic on his face. He was ankle deep in water. 'I said I would come with you, and I shall. I'm not afraid, Caylen, I'm truly not. I shall cross the river and we'll run together, just like we always said.'

He came deeper, and the river rose against him. There were tears in his eyes, and the fear on his face grew visibly as he went towards the rapids. Behind him the men who had killed the stranger watched in silence, fearful for the boy's life, yet puzzled as to the courage of the lad, a courage that made him risk his life in the foulest waters they had ever seen.

'Oh Fergus, no ... you *must* listen to me. Go back, *please!* Don't follow me, don't give me away ... go *back!*'

But the boy came on, fear overwhelming reason, courage and the pursuit of honour blinding him to Caylen's panic, deafening him to the terrible words of his lifelong friend.

And Caylen saw that soon every man on the bank would know the illusion for what it was, and then there would be no haven for the boy, no place of refuge for the ghost of a girl that might one day spirit the life back into a people as distant and as alien from Caylen as were his own people.

And yet to stop him, to stop him ... such a decision, such a tearing of heart and mind, to sacrifice his friend for the sake of freedom. And even then it was not resolved. For how could Caylen save himself except by using that same spear which was a symbol of peace, of compassion, everything that might make a nation great in greater times than these?

Even as he thought this, the stark images of the stranger's story became vivid again – the killing, the running, the cold-blooded murder of an hysterical girl by a man paid to do the deed, a man whom remorse, some awareness of the beauty he had killed, had changed from mercenary to guardian. He had run with the spear, creating in his own mind the legend of a supernatural presence in the blade. But there had been no magic, Caylen realised. The spear, a cold, dead weapon, was all that remained of her. It was the horn-helmeted man himself who threatened those who pursued him, a man with a memory that needed obliteration. He was dead now, and the weapon was just a weapon. Whether it was destroyed or not, whatever memory of Rianna remained in that far-off land would be the same. This spear, or another, what mattered were the words that spoke the legend.

Old enough to grasp this simple truth, Caylen was too young to realise that the illusion of hope was best served by less complex symbols. He flung the spear back to the far shore and watched as the strangers destroyed it. By the time Fergus had waded to the nearer shore, face aglow with triumph, the strangers were gone.

Caylen turned from his friend and walked quickly away from the river.

Once a scientist involved in secret research (just like characters in his recent humorous novel *The Leaky Establishment*) and the author of the non-fiction title *War in 2080: The Future of Military Technology*, Reading-based David Langford now writes full-time. His first novel, *The Space Eater*, appeared in 1982. Although set in a domain reminiscent of the high fantasy of, say, Jessica Salmonson's story, his short tale has a cosmological sting in the tail that makes it eminently suitable to close this anthology on a puzzling note.

In the Place of Power

David Langford

It had been cold at first, when Tirion climbed above the clouds.
White ridges and peaks towered ahead, hard-edged and perfect
against the sky's unearthly blue, almost painful to the eye. To
descend again through those puffy clouds to the softness of the
valley ... after this it would be like wallowing in mud, Tirion
thought, exalted. It had been cold at first, each breath scouring
his throat and nostrils like splintered ice: but now it seemed less
so. He climbed on, gloved hands fumbling for purchase on the
treacherous slope, towards the topmost peak and the place of
power.

'Can you hear me coming, Magus? Can you hear me coming?'
he whispered.

The mountains which ringed the one valley were called the
edge of the world; they might be or they might not; nobody knew
what was beyond. Once the world – the valley – had been larger,
perhaps hundreds of miles across rather than a puny five; but
lately the edges of the world were closing in. By night or even by
day, the foothills would shuffle inward. Another farm, another
family, would be gone. Even day and night were not the reliable
things they had been. The brightest summer afternoon might be
disfigured by an hour-long patch of night, or the hues of sunset
swallowed in a wholly improper dawn. It was not to be tolerated.
There were dreams and visions, signs and portents, as always, as
ever. Appalling things stalked the darkness, as though demanding propitiation. The word 'sacrifice' was mentioned rather too
soon and rather too frequently for Tirion's liking – he knew that
his own burning ambition and manoeuvres for power were
resented. And sure enough, with much flattery of his youth,
strength and cleverness, the village fathers chose Tirion for the
ostensible task of pleading with the legendary Magus in his place
of power. None of them dwelt on the tradition that people had

gone that way before, or the lack of any tradition relating to their return.

Tirion had his own ideas about sacrifice, and he carried a well-sharpened knife. With keen wits and a keen knife, he considered, a man might steal treasure or power even from a Magus.

The last part of the ascent was the easiest. By now it was neither warm nor cold; he felt buoyed up by the calm sea of air, rising almost effortlessly like a bubble in clear water. Nearing the summit, he staggered and shook his head. The rugged shoulders of the mountain converged but carried no final peak: something had sheared the problematical peak away to leave a smooth surface like a mirror of ice, crackling with the clear blue of the sky. Though visibly tilted towards him and the valley below, the ten or twenty gleaming acres held Tirion's eye and told it that somehow this mirror was truly level, the rest of the world askew. So he stumbled. Even having seen the trick, if it was a trick, he felt continuing waves of giddiness there at the edge of the place of power.

Over the gleaming blue a dark blot moved towards him like a spider. It was a man, a ragged man who walked the slope as though it were truly as level as it pretended, as level as calm water – and as though the upright Tirion were leaning ludicrously forward.

'Magus,' Tirion said, sliding a hand down his right leg to what was in his boot, his mind a churning stew of ambition and fear.

The man shrugged. His black beard was full and his face unlined, but the voice creaked like old and rusty machinery. 'Magus? I don't think of myself by that name; or any other, as it happens. No, leave the knife alone, you won't need it. I promise you. Let me think. Your name would be Tirion. Brown hair. Yes.'

Tirion teased out a lock of his hair and squinted at it. 'Yesterday it was yellow, the day before it was black – what does it matter?'

'I apologise. My abilities are failing. This is why you are here.'

'I don't understand,' said Tirion, beginning to wonder if this might be a mere madman.

'That too is why you are here. There are important turns of

history which you and the valleyfolk have never known – also a certain point of geography. Come, and I'll show you what lies beyond the mountains.'

'Will I ... will I be able to go back down after?'

'You'll see all your friends again before the day is over. Now come with me ... no, don't cross the border of the Place, not now. Around the edge to the other side of the mountain, the side which doesn't look down into your valley. I'll walk with you, you on your ground and I on mine.'

They walked, the Magus (if that was what he was) gliding over the impossibly perfect mirror while Tirion toiled up rock and shale an arm's length away. To look to his left and the 'Place' meant vertigo; indeed, to look anywhere but where his feet were going meant a likely fall ...

'Stop now,' said a rusty voice. Just ahead the pathway ended in blue sky. Tirion glanced at his guide, who was staring back with a critical frown. 'Red hair?'

Again Tirion peered at a loose lock of his own hair. 'Red, yes. Changed again since we started walking. Does it matter?'

'It matters very much indeed. This is not the way things should be. Again, my apologies. Now what did I bring you here for? Something you had to know ...'

'The other side of the mountain.'

'Quite. I would have remembered in a moment. Take a pace or two forward, then, very carefully if you please, and look over the edge.'

Tirion did this. There was a long pause. He could find no words for what he saw. The bright horror beyond the world made the disorienting ways of the place of power seem nothing. Looking down, he saw that there was no such thing as a level surface, no straight line or right angle anywhere, no solid matter or empty air, no laws or words or reasons or –

'Tirion.'

If only he stared long enough he would know the secrets beyond knowledge, beyond good and evil, beyond thought.

'*Tirion*. Close your eyes.'

The whiplash of authority in the order struck through. Tirion shut his eyes, put his hands to his face, swayed on the brink, assaulted by monstrous after-images.

'Now turn around ... That's right. Sit down.'

He was sitting on a rock he didn't remember being there, blinking in thin sunlight. The man with the black beard and old eyes watched him, his expression compounded of kindliness and distraction.

'*That* is what lies beyond the mountains. It presses inward, but so far it does not prevail – not since the beginning. Did I say I would tell you history? I'll tell it now.

'Longer ago than I like to think or you could comprehend, the maker conceived the world. That was the beginning. They still tell the story, don't they? Yes. The maker imagined the world in all its detail, imagined it with a force that pushed back – what you saw. You'll have listened to your village philosopher, maybe, saying that nothing exists save as a thought in the mind of the maker. Sophistry, you might have thought, if you knew the word. Not at all ...'

'I know it,' Tirion muttered. Babbling old fool, he thought.

'Good. Where was I? The maker sat in the place of power, holding the world's image in his mind, and all was well. Her mind, its mind? It could have been any or all three. All *this* –' indicating the bare waste of mirror – 'was the maker's notion of a comfortable seat, a niche, a resting-place ...

'Then after an uncounted time the maker's attention turned elsewhere, to greater things perhaps, and all the world began to change and to decay. As it faded from the maker's mind it faded altogether ... all the same, here we are now, eh? Now why is that?

'Ah yes. Before the real things – the things outside – could squeeze our world away, a man climbed to the place of power. He was only a man and not the maker, but he held the world in his mind and preserved it as best he could. But still, he was only a man, and for all the power of the place he grew old.'

'*You?*'

'Not I. He was the Magus. In the Place he needed no food nor drink, which was fortunate. He kept his strength, more fortunate still. Sleep, though, he could never do without sleep, and when he slept the world went dark. In the days of the maker there was no night, you know? And, and, what was the next thing ... his mind began to shrivel. He would forget. The tiniest of things at first, a dewdrop, a blade of grass, a stray toadstool or a pebble on the stream's bed. Nobody would know or care if these slipped from the mind of the Magus and from the world. Then, perhaps, matters more noticeable. The colour of a boy's hair. A whole pasture or spinney at the foot of the mountains. And in the end, who knows?'

He was looking very hard at Tirion, who said: 'You. It must be you. My hair . . .'

'The world is older than you think. I am the ninety-fourth successor of the Magus. But yes: lately I've begun to forget things.'

'And our world grows smaller?'

'Quite.'

'The other thing – the night that comes by noon or the dawn in the evening?'

The old man who did not look old smiled. 'Another curse of age. In spite of all my discipline I fall asleep when I shouldn't, wake when I should sleep: night comes, or light – you see the way of it. And horrid things walk the night for you, don't they? I'm sorry. Lately, I have bad dreams. – Now take my hand.'

Again the sudden iron of command in his tone made Tirion obey without thought: his hand rose to encounter the man's strong grip, and he was pulled with a jerk to his feet.

'No,' he said as an appalling realisation came to him. He tried to step back; his free hand groped awkwardly for the knife.

'What – ? Oh, you had something in your boot, didn't you? Some sort of weapon.' A sardonic chuckle. 'I'm afraid I've forgotten what it was.'

And the knife was no longer there.

'I must tell you one last thing,' said the ancient and now hateful rusty voice. 'One last legend. Remember it. It is said that when the holder of the place of power can imagine a vast enough world, can imagine the mountain barriers further and further away until they meet in the unthinkable distance and close off the world from the flux outside . . . on that day the Place and its prisoner will be needed no more. Perhaps then the world can be left to exist in the minds of common folk: I don't know. Remember it, though. And if you're not the one to solve that riddle, remember to imagine yourself a worthy successor in the Place – and to pass on what I've said. Let that be the last of all the things you forget.'

The painful hold on Tirion's hand tightened until he felt the bones grate; there was a tug and a moment's whirling confusion. He was standing unsteadily on the ice-mirror of the Place, which all his senses agreed was perfectly flat and sane; but the whole world outside had tilted until the toothed mountains far across the valley seemed to tower over this, the tallest of them all. A dreadful knowledge was battering on the doors of his mind.

He saw his predecessor standing at an insane angle, no longer within the Place, the man seemed suddenly older, lined and bent, his beard streaked with cloudy grey. 'Goodbye. And good luck.' Then the former Magus turned, took two firm paces to the world's edge, and was gone. To final forgetfulness, perhaps, or to forge his own world rather than sniff like a dog at the Maker's leavings: there was no way to tell, not yet.

The dreadful knowledge was swarming through Tirion now, funnelling into him like endless grains of sand, the knowledge of all the world focused by the place of power, the million million weights and numbers, tastes and colours, moods and whims which made up the sum of things which were. He saw it all in the mirror underfoot; he knew it all, and it was his duty to remember it all. And more.

You'll see all your friends again before the day is over. Tirion saw them and knew them through and through, and it was not enough.

He remembered the knife, and felt its welcome presence again in his boot. It would be easy to end everything – but he could not do that to the world that danced in the mirror and in his mind, aglitter with such overwhelming detail. Probably he'd been chosen as someone who would not do that. Or created as someone who would not. His own ambition, if nothing else, would hold him prisoner. The numb weight of responsibility and of all the things there were pressed down on him.

He clenched his fists in futile anger, and great thunderheads boiled up in the valley far below. He screwed up his eyes, and bitter rain broke from the clouds like tears. In long rolls of thunder he cried out against the unfairness of it all, that he should be burdened with this omnipotence and throned at the top of the world, in the place of power.